CREDIT CRUNCHIES

Bite-size quotes from your favourite politicians, bankers and others

WILL HANAFIN

POOLBEG

Happy Birthday Fergal,
I'm sure you'll
feature in the
next political
publication...

Denny
'09

Published 2009
by Poolbeg Books Ltd.
123 Grange Hill, Baldoyle,
Dublin 13, Ireland
Email: poolbeg@poolbeg.com

13 5 7 9 10 8 6 4 2

A catalogue record for this book is available from the British Library.

ISBN 978-1-84223-422-8

Cover design and illustrations by Derry Dillon
Typeset by Patrica Hope in Myriad Pro 10/13
Printed by
Litografia Rosés S.A., Spain

www.poolbeg.com

About the Author

Will Hanafin is a writer and broadcaster. He produces the Ray D'Arcy Show on Today FM and also steps up to the mike occasionally. He is also a writer with the *Sunday Independent*, writing features for *Life* Magazine and contributing to the *Living* supplement. Will is the author of four previous books including the bestselling *De Little Book of Bertie* about the odd utterances of our former Taoiseach. He's married to Mary Kirwan and has one son Ethan.

Contents

Introduction   1

I Told You So Crunchies   5

Irish Banking Crunchies   21

Irish Political Crunchies   46

Hopelessly Optimistic Crunchies   74

Contrite Crunchies   90

Villainous Crunchies   111

Celebrity Crunchies   121

Seriously Funny Crunchies   133

Global Banking Crunchies   159

Global Political Crunchies   174

To Mary and Ethan, with all my love.

Introduction

What are credit crunchies? They're quotes or sentences that sum up the crisis we find ourselves in right now. They can be uttered by politicians, bankers and others – mainly people who caused this economic mess but don't want to take responsibility.

Sometimes credit crunchies will make you laugh; sometimes they might make you cry. Some might even make you cry with laughter. Credit crunchies are funny and they're serious – but mainly they're seriously funny. Laughter is really the best reaction to the traumatic events of the last two years.

Many credit crunchies highlight the financial crisis as the biggest case of "I told you so!" since Spike Milligan had the words "I told you I was sick" chiselled on his gravestone.

The politicians and bankers who got it so wrong keep telling us that a stopped clock is right twice a day – so consequently nobody could really have predicted what happened. The Irish Government were told to put the brakes on as early as 2003 by *The Economist* magazine. Here's one of several quotes from them:

> *"If the housing bubbles burst, the economic consequences will be much more severe than those of the recent stock market crash, because more households own homes than own shares, and because home-owners are up to their necks in debt."*

The IMF also raised the spectre of a property crash in 2006.

"At this point, concerns centre on the United States although other markets, such as those in Ireland, Spain and the UK, still seem overvalued by most conventional measures."

But the bankers and the politicians didn't want to deflate the bubble. Instead, shamed Anglo Irish Bank boss Sean Fitzpatrick obsessed about too much regulation in 2005. Well, turkeys aren't the biggest fans of Christmas either!

"The pronounced moves towards greater control and regulation could squeeze the life out of an economy that has thrived on intuition, imagination and a spirit of adventure."

The bankers gloated about their salaries. Brian Goggin of Bank of Ireland wanted sympathy for his salary of "less than two million. Sean Fitzpatrick thought we all loved him because he was raking in millions:

"I've had no overt negative criticism at all about how much I'm paid. Strangely perhaps for Irish people, most people have said well done."

Fitzpatrick was ungracious to the end. This is what he said on radio when the government launched the bank guarantee scheme.

"I can't say sorry with any degree of sincerity and decency, but I do say thank you."

Politicians were asleep on their watch but because they're still in power they refuse to say sorry or, more worryingly, to learn from their mistakes. In 2006 Mary Harney rubbished reports that the housing sector was in trouble.

"The consensus scenario for the housing market is a soft landing . . ."

Vested interests like the property supplements also kept cheerleading for the construction industry. Here's a quote from the *Irish Times* property supplement in 2004:

"Despite all the doom and gloom warnings by the Central Bank and The Economist *magazine . . . there is no sign of the Irish property "bubble" bursting any time soon . . ."*

Our leaders even started getting cocky. Far from apologising for his running of the economy, in 2006 Bertie Ahern wanted economic forecasters to say sorry to him because the economy didn't collapse that year.

"Really we should have an examination into why so many people got it so wrong. My view is there's not a great problem. Really, the bad advice of last year given by so many has maybe made some people make mistakes, that they should have bought last year."

On Budget Day 2007, our then Finance Minister Brian Cowen said there was no need to call a halt to our out-of-control growth.

"A measured deceleration is required, not a sudden slamming of brakes."

When the brakes were applied for us, nobody took the blame. Brian Lenihan told us the bleeding obvious.

"With the benefit of hindsight it is clear that more should have been done to contain the housing market."

Brian Cowen was at sea – or blaming something called an "economic tsunami". Here's his solution back in February:

". . . Taking some steps back so we can go forward again."

Cowen blamed other people for bad advice:

"I take all the responsibility for all of the decisions that I have taken. They were taken by me on the basis of the best possible advice available to me at the time."

He bemoaned his lack of balls – and so did we!

"Of course, there'd be different decisions that you would take. But we don't all have crystal balls."

At least there's humour, as the US chat show hosts like Jay Leno have had a great recession:

"The United States have developed a new weapon that destroys people but it leaves buildings standing. It's called the stock market."

Then there are the anonymous gags about the recession that have flooded the internet:

"The credit crunch has helped me get back on my feet. The car's been repossessed."

"How do you define optimism? A banker who irons five shirts on a Sunday."

There's a credit crunchie in here for everyone! Enjoy!

Will Hanafin

I Told You So Crunchies

They were right all along – damn them!

2003

Bubble trouble ahead

"The Irish housing market is currently in the early stages of an asset bubble. While we are likely to see ongoing price rises . . . of the order of 8% year-on-year, we are increasingly concerned about the overall stability of the market."

Colin Hunt, the chief economist at Goodbody Stockbrokers, spells it out pretty clearly six years ago.   30 March 2003

Pre-emptive strike

"In a world of near-zero inflation, double-digit returns are no more sustainable on houses than on equities. Next time an exuberant estate agent tells you that bricks and mortar are the safest thing you can invest in, hit him on the head with this copy of The Economist.*"*

The first clear warning about our overheating housing market from a respected magazine – and the green light to assault an auctioneer!   *The Economist*, 31 May 2003

Bubble, bubble, toil and trouble

"If the housing bubbles burst, the economic consequences will be much more severe than those of the recent stock market crash, because more households own homes than own shares, and because home-owners are up to their necks in debt."

Put the brakes on NOW, Bertie!　　*The Economist*, 31 May 2003

Blowing our bubble

"With the global economy already so fragile . . . the result will be uncomfortable at best – and painful at worst. But that is what happens when bubbles are blown up and burst."

It felt like the government were just blowing bubbles six years ago – rather than doing their job!

The Economist, 31 May 2003

Don't do it!

"Anyone thinking of buying in any of the housing markets that this survey has identified as bubbling should wait until prices have fallen."

A clear shout out to "get away from the estate agents now!"

The Economist, 31 May 2003

The fall guys

"Anyone who already owns a home but has to move for work or family reasons should consider selling and renting until prices drop. Most home-owners, however, will have to stick it out and watch their wealth dwindle. Their mistake was not to buy a home, because they can still enjoy living there. Where they went wrong was in expecting double-digit returns to continue . . ."

That's telling us! But did we listen . . . uh-uh!

The Economist, 31 May 2003

Mystic Shane

"The Central Bank is worried, The Economist *magazine fears a collapse. Yet the banks are still shovelling money at borrowers. Auctioneers are encouraging people to pay crazy prices.*

Mortgage lending is growing by 24 per cent per annum. I foresee tears for the punters, riches for the auctioneers and ruthless repossessions by the banks. God forgive them."

Shane Ross certainly has a fully functioning crystal ball. What a man!

Sunday Independent, 10 August 2003

We should have listened . . .

"It would take a brave person – be they a renowned economist, a leading estate agent or a crystal ball-gazing fortune teller – to instruct anybody who has to sell their home to hold off buying a new house and rent until prices drop.

It would take an equally courageous person to tell a financially-strapped first-time buyer with loan approval looking for a house or apartment they can just about afford now to postpone their house hunt, continue renting and wait for a couple of years before buying when prices will probably be lower. This is, however, exactly what The Economist *magazine has done in its survey of housing prices . . . as they predict that housing prices in Ireland will fall by 20% in the next four years – and . . . as much as 44% in some areas."*

Helen Rogers spells out the big ask in the *Sunday Tribune*.

1 June 2003

Explosive predictions

"Derivatives are financial weapons of mass destruction, carrying dangers that, while now latent, are potentially lethal."

Renowned investor Warren Buffett's warning in 2003 that derivatives are the devil's work. Derivatives – financial contracts whose values are derived from something else – were at the heart of the credit crunch.

BBC News, 4 March 2003

Talking sense

"People should not be foolish enough to take up 100% financing when it looks like we're coming to the end of the property boom. You've got to remember that your life can change quickly so you may need to sell your house before you'd planned. This won't be possible if you're trapped in negative equity."

Sensible financial advice in the *Sunday Tribune*.

25 May 2003

2004

Hubba bubba!

"In the past three years, the total value of residential property in developed economies has increased by an estimated $20 trillion, to over $60 trillion . . . double the $10 trillion by which global share values climbed in the three years to 1999. Is this the biggest financial bubble in history?"

It's 2004 and *The Economist* is still worried.

11 December 2004

Swings and roundabouts

"Just as the current upswing in housing prices has largely been a global phenomenon, any downturn is also likely to be highly synchronised across countries, with corresponding implications for the world economy."

And so is the International Monetary Fund. Here's what they say in the *IMF Research Bulletin*.

The Irish Times, 23 September 2004

2005

The king of pops

"The worldwide rise in house prices is the biggest bubble in history. Prepare for the economic pain when it pops."

The tension is becoming unbearable at this stage!

The Economist, 18 June 2005

Bang!

"Never before have real house prices risen so fast for so long in so many countries ... Measured by the increase in asset values over the past five years, the global housing boom is the biggest financial bubble in history. The bigger the boom, the bigger the eventual bust."

The Economist report, June 2005

More tension!

"The air is slowly leaking from the global housing bubble."

At least someone is releasing the pressure!

The Economist, 10 December 2005

2006

Asleep on the job

"House prices may have overshot, the survey says, and house-building will eventually slow. A prudent government should create fiscal room now to cushion a possible hard landing later . . ."

Fiscal room? Most of our TDs probably think it's a suite in Buswell's Hotel! *The Economist* commenting on the latest OECD economic survey of Ireland.   18 March 2006

Ice house

"A key risk on the demand side is that continued cooling of advanced economies' housing markets will weaken household balance sheets and undercut aggregate demand. At this point, concerns centre on the US, although other markets, such as those in Ireland, Spain and the United Kingdom, also still seem overvalued by most conventional measures."

The IMF gets involved again and addresses their concerns in a report.   *The Independent*, 14 September 2006

School of hard knocks

"Descartes . . . said education is often and necessarily painful. Alas, if pain is necessary to teach that the present property explosion is a bubble, there will be an awful lot of tears before bedtime. It may be that preparing people for the end of the housing price boom . . . will be the biggest political challenge in the next five or ten years."

Journalist Martin Fitzpatrick recommends some advance preparation. *Sunday Independent*, 16 July 2006

Flexible forecasts

"We can be sure in Ireland something unexpected is going to happen, so the key will be how flexible we are and how we respond to that."

Economist Alan Aherne tells us to expect the unexpected back in 2006, reported in *Press Association Newsfile*.

7 April 2009

Excellent call

"My own view . . . is that the more likely trigger for the next downturn will be something happening to house prices worldwide. There is an element of 'bubble' to prices in many markets (as the new IMF Economic Outlook acknowledges)."

Hamish McRae calls it right in the *Sunday Tribune*.

17 September 2006

Corrective inaction

"An 'abrupt correction' to the property market cannot be ruled out."

The IMF's annual report on Ireland in *The Irish Times*.

8 August 2006

Each way bet!

"40% of house-price booms end in busts . . . there is a clear risk of a disruptive adjustment and a global recession . . ."

Another IMF report giving us some really big hints!

The Daily Mail, 20 April 2006

Rare warning!

"The pick-up in house prices is a worrying development and increases the risk of a sharp correction."

Tom O'Connell, the Assistant Director General of the Central Bank, with a timely warning.   *Sunday Tribune*, 7 May 2006

Getting it off your chest

"The combination of artificially low interest rates, foreign central bank intervention, an irresponsible Fed, excessive credit availability, the proliferation of low or no-down payment, adjustable-rate, interest-only . . . mortgages, a can't-lose attitude among speculators . . . the complete abandonment of lending standards, widespread corruption in the appraisal industry, rampant fraud among sub-prime lenders and the moral hazards associated with loan originators reselling loans to buyers of securitised products who perceive minimal risk and an implied government guarantee, has produced the mother of all bubbles."

It may be a mouthful but American broker Peter Schiff calls it right back in 2006!   *The Stamford Advocate*, 6 August 2006

"Chairman Bernanke is whistling past
the graveyard if he thinks that the
housing recession is not going to negatively
affect consumer spending via declining
mortgage equity withdrawal."

Paul Kasriel

2007

But who's listening?

"Ireland looks rockier still. House building accounts directly for a staggering 15% of national income and 12% of employment. Whereas prices have soared, rents have stagnated in recent years and, at 4%, rental yields in Dublin do not cover even the cost of borrowing. Now prices are flattening too."

The Economist valiantly tries one more time!

24 March 2007

Grave concerns

"[US Federal Reserve Board] Chairman [Ben] Bernanke is whistling past the graveyard if he thinks that the housing recession is not going to negatively affect consumer spending via declining mortgage equity withdrawal."

Paul Kasriel, Director of Economic Research for Northern Trust in Chicago.   *The Sunday Times*, 12 August 2007

At last!

"Ireland's long housing boom has turned to bust. Prices fell by almost 3% in the 12 months to September; a year earlier, house-price inflation was above 15%."

The Economist finally gets its moment of glory!

8 December 2007

Crash!

"The overstretched, overleveraged financial system is a slow-motion train wreck . . . the first truly global bubble in asset prices will cause one major bank to fail."

US fund manager Jeremy Grantham warning in 2007 that it was all going to end in tears.

Quoted in *The Irish Times*, 8 August 2008

Steady Eddie

"My advice to first-time buyers is not to buy. They should rent for the next year or 24 months. There's no doubt that property prices will continue to go down and if they save though an institution like Northern Rock they will have capital in the future when prices are lower."

Eddie Hobbs urges us to save our pennies.

Irish Independent, 21 April 2007

2008

Suitably vague

"To say that the backdrop is 'recession-like' is akin to an obstetrician telling a woman that she is 'sort of pregnant'."

This Merrill Lynch report flags that the US has plunged towards recession. But back in January 2008 the National Bureau of Economic Research – the only body that officially decides whether it's a recession – is keeping quiet.

The Irish Times, 11 January 2008

The man's a prophet!

"The international credit crunch will have a knock-on effect on the whole economy."

Eddie Hobbs is really some forecaster!

The Irish Times, 4 October 2008

Piggy flu bank

Many investors still believe that the credit crisis is purely a US subprime problem. Nothing could be further from the truth . . . There appears to be a growing global credit pandemic."

Merrill Lynch's chief investment strategist, Richard Bernstein, has got a pretty direct bedside manner when it comes to the world's money markets.

The Irish Times, 25 January 2008

Whopper fried!

"We're not just going to see mid-sized banks go under in the next few months, we're going to see a whopper."

The prediction of the year by Harvard Professor Kenneth Rogoff, the former chief economist of the International Monetary Fund. He made this forecast in August 2008; just over two weeks later, Lehman Brothers went bankrupt.

Quoted in *The Independent*, 1 January 2009

Irish Banking Crunchies

Bonuses, Bail outs and Bankers

Control freak out

"The pronounced moves towards greater control and regulation could squeeze the life out of an economy that has thrived on intuition, imagination and a spirit of adventure."

Disgraced Anglo Irish Bank boss Sean Fitzpatrick freaks about control and regulation of the banking sector during a 2005 speech.

What regulation?

"Financial regulation in the State was a joke."

Senator Shane Ross following the revelation that Sean Fitzpatrick had €87 million in hidden loans at Anglo Irish Bank.

Cracking up

"A building society on crack."

One London fund manager's description of Anglo Irish
Bank.   *The Sunday Times*, 15 February 2009

Prudent risk taking

*"Banking ultimately . . . is about prudence – but it is also about
risk taking. Banks take risks."*

Ex-Bank of Ireland chief executive Brian Goggin is clearly in
two minds.   *RTÉ News*, February 2009

Prudent prudence

*"Banking is ultimately about prudence and conservatism. The
US sub-prime blow-out is the result of utter disregard for both
of these."*

Bank of Ireland's Brian Goggin attempts the moral high
ground approach – before the moral high ground collapsed
beneath him.   *Irish Independent*, 29 May 2008

Risky strategy

"I never saw us take a big risk at all. Of course there is a risk in lending but never a huge risk."

Anglo Irish chairman Sean Fitzpatrick quoted in the book *Achievers* (Oak Tree Press, 2005).

Slowdown millionaire

"The slowdown is no bad thing. It causes all of us to pull up our socks. Success isn't our automatic right. We have to continue to earn it."

Brian Goggin, the Bank of Ireland CEO, socks it to us as the recession begins to bite last year.   29 May 2008

The ultimate sacrifice

"It will be less than two million."

Bank of Ireland chief executive Brian Goggin will be able to afford very expensive socks to pull up with a salary like that.
RTÉ News, February 2009

"If Bank of Ireland is the David Niven of banking, AIB is the Gene Hackman and Anglo Irish is the Del Boy."

Indecent exposure

"We have exposure to hotels, pubs and investment properties . . . we are not exposed fully to the economic vagaries of those sectors because our investment is in their bricks and mortar."

Anglo Irish Bank boss Sean Fitzpatrick reassures us all back in 2002 but forgets that the bricks and mortar might also drop in value. Ah, 20/20 hindsight!   *Business and Finance*, 2002

Only fools!

"If Bank of Ireland is the David Niven of banking, AIB is the Gene Hackman and Anglo Irish is the Del Boy."

An anonymous banker quoted in the book *Banksters* (Hodder Headline Ireland 2009).

Future shock

"It is absolutely correct that where serious wrong-doing has been uncovered it should be exposed."

Even back in 2005 Anglo Irish Bank boss Sean Fitzpatrick was concerned about future exposure!

Arrogant? Moi?

"On occasions the confidence that fuelled much of the business dynamism turned to arrogance."

Humble, understated Anglo Irish Bank chairman Sean Fitzpatrick reviews the downside of business success in a 2005 speech.

Bank to the future

"We can't in any way afford to be complacent as the economy slows down. But we know that in that scenario, people will actually deal more with an experienced niche bank like ourselves, because we can provide them with a more tailored service."

Modest Anglo Irish bank boss Sean Fitzpatrick tries his hand at predicting the future . . . Leave it to the professionals, we say!
Business and Finance, 2002

Broken vows

"We had to pull up all the floorboards and re-examine the business. It prompted a fundamental rethink and that's been good for the bank. We renewed our vows that we were not going to be found wanting again in any respect."

Donal Forde, the managing director of AIB in the Republic of Ireland, speaking in late 2007. He obviously missed a few floorboards. *Irish Independent*, 8 November 2007

Credibility limit

"Every day some bank comes out with a howler. Banks have destroyed their credibility to a very significant degree over the last six months."

AIB chief executive Eugene Sheehy comes out with the howler that the woes of banks only started six months earlier.   *The Irish Times*, 22 February 2008

Recession buster

"We got out of jail in the late 1980s . . . but we now have an entrepreneurial culture and flair and have accumulated wealth we never had in the past."

Bank of Ireland boss Brian Goggin plans to fight the economic downturn with flair back in May 2008. Good luck to you!   *Irish Independent*, 29 May 2008

Target driven

"During the boom lots of people saw their credit card limits as targets rather than limits!"

Eddie Hobbs stretches us all to our limits with his dinner party one-liners.

From robust to go bust

"I think the Irish housing market is an important component of the economy, but it is by no means the whole story. The Irish economy is very resilient and very robust."

Denis Casey, chief executive of Irish Life and Permanent.

The Irish Times, 31 August 2007

Fasten your seat belts

"The annual rate of house price inflation could well turn negative over the summer months ... Thus, we are now forecasting an end year inflation rate of minus 2%, which would still constitute a soft landing."

AIB are on the money as usual about the Irish property market in a quote from their June 2007 housing market bulletin.

The Irish Times, 8 June 2007

It'll blow over

"All things being equal, [the credit market turmoil] should be a temporary phenomenon."

Robert Gallagher, the chief executive of Ulster Bank Corporate Markets, may need to get his crystal ball serviced!

Irish Independent, 18 October 2007

Oh, yes you do!

"We are not all the same. AIB has made it clear we don't feel we need capital."

Donal Forde, the head of AIB's operations in Ireland, speaking to an Oireachtas committee. Since then the state has had to inject €3.5 billion into AIB – and it says it needs €1.5 billion more. *The Irish Times*, 17 December 2008

Quacking up

"The whole board should be replaced by Mickey Mouse and Donald Duck . . . we should go to Disneyland in Paris."

AIB shareholder Gary Keogh has some ideas about the new board. There's no place for a duck on the AIB board – we've been presented with enough large bills from them already! *Irish Examiner*, 14 May 2009

You don't say!

"The real mistake, for which I take responsibility, is that we lent too much for development land in Ireland."

Pity it took so long but AIB boss Eugene Sheehy finally figures it out with this eureka moment.

The Irish Times, 14 May 2009

Famous last words

"We'd rather die than raise equity . . ."

AIB chief executive Eugene Sheehy exposes his inner drama queen as the banking crisis worsens.

Business World, 24 October 2008

Dead duck

"Mr Eugene Sheehy said that he would prefer to die than recapitalise the bank . . . Well what's stopping him? . . . He can die any day of the week and the rest of the board."

Eugene Sheehy's words come back to haunt him. AIB shareholder Gary Keogh's comments after throwing an egg at chairman Dermot Gleeson.   Today FM news, 13 May 2009

Tie anxiety

"I don't want to expose anyone else to an egg on the suit or egg on the tie. I think the tie escaped."

The AIB chairman Dermot Gleeson worries about the important things in life after being pelted with an egg.

The Irish Times, 14 May 2009

No it isn't! They're back!

"Many of us will remember the mid-1970s to the mid-1980s. It's easy, though, to forget the days of negative growth, high unemployment, high taxation, high interest rates, rampant emigration and balance of payment problems."

Sean Fitzpatrick switches from the ghost of Christmas past to the ghost of Christmas future with ease back in September 2005.

Oh no you're not!

"We are a well capitalised bank. I believe the decision made last Monday [for the state guarantee scheme] is probably the most important decision made, from an economic point of view, since the foundation of the state."

Anglo chairman Sean Fitzpatrick spins a yarn last October on RTÉ's *Marian Finucane Show*. In May 2009 Anglo Irish Bank reported a loss of €4 billion. The bank has impaired loan charges of €4.1 billion, which may rise to €7.5 billon.

Fewer laws . . . hmmm!

"We do not need more legislation. What we really need is fewer laws, but which are better and more stringently enforced."

Anglo Irish boss Sean Fitzpatrick back in 2005. Now he would say that, wouldn't he?!

Give it a couple of years . . .

"We're moving towards regulatory and compliance barriers that are significantly more stringent than two of our most important trading partners. But why? What has been done here over the past decade that demands such a reaction? Where is the line-up of failed companies with shareholders who've been ripped-off and left bemoaning the lack of due care and attention by feckless directors?"

Sean Fitzpatrick should have been careful what he wished for back in 2005.

The great deceiver

"Sean Fitzpatrick deceived, when he was chief executive and chairman, his board, shareholders, general public and staff."

The Financial Services Ombudsman, Joe Meade.

TV3, 15 January 2009

Mad hatter

"You have to appoint someone who is the devil's advocate on a management team and change their hats every now and then so you don't have a Dr Gloom or a Dr Good Times."

Hats off to new Bank of Ireland chief Richie Boucher for letting us have an insight into his mind.

The Irish Times, 22 May 2009

Strange brew

"We drank too deeply from the national cup of confidence . . . the national mood of self confidence brewed itself up into overdrive."

AIB chairman Dermot Gleeson finally reveals what they were on all that time. *The Irish Times*, 14 May 2009

Financial windfall

"The top brass in AIB should be welded to wind turbines to stand as rotating monuments to our national greed."

AIB shareholder Frank Mockler has put just a little too much thought into this suggestion to improve the company. Wind farm owners, you have been warned.

The Irish Times, 14 May 2009

For all the wrong reasons

"And all the time as we worked the scene and maximised the moment, the world watched in astonishment."

Sean Fitzpatrick reminisces about the Celtic Tiger back in 2005. Strangely prophetic because the world is still looking at us in astonishment – and I don't mean that in a good way!

Headline grabber

"Irish stand united in hatred of this man."

Headline in *USA Today* newspaper following Sean Fitzpatrick's fall from grace.

Accentuate the positive

"It remains the case that many in the business press seem always to focus on the negative."

Anglo Irish's Sean Fitzpatrick tries to eliminate the negative in 2005.

We were right!

"What I see from where I am sitting, is a general acceptance by most of the media that business is dodgy or suspect and it needs to be highly regulated."

Sean Fitzpatrick tempts fate by blaming the media for bad impressions of the business sector in 2005.

Ageing badly

"We've come from a position of childhood, through adolescence and young adulthood. We haven't fully matured yet, I would accept that, but I'd also hasten to add that we've seen no sign of deterioration in our asset quality out there."

Sean Fitzpatrick compares Anglo Irish Bank to an irresponsible young buck. He could just be right for once!

Business and Finance, 2002

Time wasters

"We would put in whatever hours and whatever miles it required to take those ideas and turn them into business successes."

Maybe nine-to-five would have saved everyone a lot of bother. Sean Fitzpatrick telling us how it was done in 2005.

Pyramid scheme

"Ireland saw the biggest building boom since the pyramids and this is going to be a painful adjustment."

Yes but all we're left with is the bloody Spire! Economist Professor Willem Buiter.   *The Irish Times*, 14 May 2009

Optimistic Meg!

"There is a massacre about to happen in the IFSC that is going to make Dell look like a birthday party."

UCD economist Morgan Kelly makes the grim reaper sound cheery as he predicts big job losses in the financial sector.
The Irish Times, 16 January 2009

Icy forecast

"The global financial crisis may have stopped us dragging ourselves even deeper into our hole. If it had taken another year or two, we would have ended up in an Icelandic-shaped hole, which is not to say that we won't end up in one [anyway]".

Economist Morgan Kelly spreads the cheer once again.
Sunday Tribune, 18 January 2009

We were had

"We had ideas, and we had balls."

Anglo Irish Bank boss Sean Fitzpatrick in 2005.

New balls, please!

"All we were doing was working our balls off, doing it in a way different to other banks."

Sean Fitzpatrick talks a lot of balls. Inevitable then that his bank would make a balls of the Irish banking system. Sean Fitzpatrick interviewed in *Achievers* (Oak Tree Press, 2005)

The naked truth

"By the end of the year, we will truly know who has been swimming without trunks."

Economist Professor Willem Buiter is "brief" and to the point about ailing banks. At least he doesn't mention balls!

The Irish Times, 14 May 2009

"I don't envisage that Nama will have a tent at any famous Irish racecourse."
Brian Lenihan

What a banker!

"We now represent the safest place to deposit money in Europe."

Michael Fingleton Jnr of Irish Nationwide writes a letter to prospective investors after the introduction of the bank guarantee scheme.   *The Sunday Times*, 28 December 2008

Proper financial regulation

"Banks need a good kick up the bum occasionally."

At last some plain speaking from a politician – unfortunately he's not one of ours. Australian Finance Minister Wayne Swan believes in going down under to solve the financial crisis.   *The Sunday Times*, 12 April 2009

Ban Nama!

"I don't envisage that Nama will have a tent at any famous Irish racecourse."

Brian Lenihan has just scuppered the team-building day for officials from the National Asset Management Agency.
                              The Irish Times, 10 April 2009

Banks a lot!

"In my humble opinion, our wealth creators should be rewarded and admired, not subjected to the levels of scrutiny which known criminals would rightly find offensive."

Anglo Irish Bank chairman Sean Fitzpatrick addressing a business lunch in 2007.

Quoted in *The Sunday Tribune* 1 March 2009

Card shark

"Mr Fitzpatrick's actions are a financial three-card trick that appear to run a coach and four through the spirit, if the not the letter, of the requirements of financial reporting."

Labour Party finance spokesperson Joan Burton criticising Sean Fitzpatrick after the Anglo Irish chairman resigned following the revelation of his €87 million secret loans with the bank.   *The Mirror*, 20 December 2008

Change of tune

"We will strive to conduct all our business to the highest ethical and corporate governance standards."

New chair of Anglo Irish Bank Donal O'Connor has upped the levels of scrutiny in the aftermath of Sean Fitzpatrick's resignation in disgrace.   *Irish Independent*, 21 February 2009

Shocking statement

"Irish banks are resilient and have good shock absorption capacity to cope with the current situation."

Financial Regulator Patrick Neary speaking days before Finance Minister Brian Lenihan had to trigger the bank guarantee scheme. *The Irish Times*, 18 October 2008

Bound to fail

"You were blindfolded, you were sitting on your hands, you had your mouth gagged and you had your ears covered."

Fianna Fáil Senator Geraldine Feeney attacks the Financial Regulator at an Oireachtas committee meeting. It's probably the best explanation as to why the Regulator was so ineffective over the years.

Sunday Tribune, 18 January 2009

Smashing forecasts

"He who lives by the crystal ball soon learns to eat ground glass."

Economist Edgar Fiedler with some very timely advice.
The Irish Times, 2 January 2009

Runs on the banks

"We might be coming out the other end of the liquidity crisis in the banks ..."

Financial Regulator Patrick Neary thinks things are loosening up.   *Sunday Independent*, 25 January 2009

No smoke without fire

"There were all sorts of rumours and stories going around about the prospects for Irish banks, that they were in imminent danger of collapse ... It was unbelievable and there was nothing to ground any of this in."

The Financial Regulator Patrick Neary curses those damned rumours again! Of course, that was the real problem!
Interviewed in *The Sunday Business Post*, 11 May 2008

Confidence trickster

"We saw a risk that the ordinary punter in the street, with their money deposited in banks which were well capitalised, profitable and well run, would start to lose confidence. That worried us greatly."

Patrick Neary tells it as it ... isn't!!
The Sunday Business Post, 11 May 2008

Light touch regulation

"Fair play to you, Willie."

Internal audit report from Anglo Irish Bank alleges this is what Financial Regulator Patrick Neary said to Anglo official **Willie McAteer** on plans to manage the bank's balance sheet.

Sunday Tribune, 22 February 2009

Overexposed

"It is . . . important to point out that Irish banks have only very limited exposures to US sub-prime losses and related credit products."

Financial Regulator Patrick Neary persists with his business-as-usual attitude, which eventually led to his departure.

The Daily Mail, 19 September 2008

Bank praises regulator shocker!

"Ireland . . . has benefited from an active regulator who hasn't been shy where he has felt it necessary to sit down and have a quiet tête-à-tête with financial institutions about their lending practices . . . "

Irish Life and Permanent boss Denis Casey had lots of nice things to say about the Financial Regulator back in 2007. Of course he did! *The Irish Times*, 31 August 2007

Appearances can be deceptive

"The underlying fundamentals of the residential market continue to appear strong. The central scenario is, therefore, for a soft, rather than a hard, landing."

The Central Bank 2007 Stability Report tells us what we wanted to hear!

Central banker

"I do not have a crystal ball, but we do stress tests on the basis of models validated by the International Monetary Fund. On preliminary results, we can say Irish financial institutions are weathering a very difficult situation well."

Central Bank Governor John Hurley reassuring an Oireachtas committee in mid-2008 that everything was fine! Just fine! Quoted in *The Sunday Business Post*, 5 October 2008

Really?

"Time and again I pointed out that the interaction between an international and a domestic shock could have serious consequences for the economy . . ."

Central Bank Governor John Hurley tells us that he told us so . . . *The Irish Times*, 16 March 2009

Wishful thinking

"We see emerging evidence now that term money is more available in the international markets than it was up to this ... That's very encouraging, and if that continues to be the case we'll see the worst of the crisis evaporating."

Financial Regulator Patrick Neary – the eternal optimist.

The Sunday Business Post, 11 May 2008

Crossed wires

"So, I'm keeping my fingers crossed. It's really only in the last two or three weeks that these more positive signs have started to emerge. I'm very encouraged by that."

It's probably okay for Financial Regulator Patrick Neary to uncross his fingers now! Doesn't seem to have done much good.

The Sunday Business Post, 11 May 2008

Gardening tips

"We shouldn't become complacent at the first sight of green shoots. There could be a harsh frost over a couple of nights that might kill off those green shoots. Let's not become overly relaxed just yet."

Financial Regulator Patrick Neary is the man to manage a herbaceous border – but regulating the banks? He's pretty chilled out back in May 2008.

The Sunday Business Post, 11 May 2008

Irish Political Crunchies

Looking for Liquidity in an Economic Tsunami

Betting scandal!

"I want to see an Ireland that backs herself."

Taoiseach Brian Cowen could get into trouble with Paddy Power for this suggestion during his Fianna Fáil Ard Fheis speech.

March 2009

Lean times

"Let us hold on to the best of ourselves and shed the rest.

Taoiseach Brian Cowen urges us all to identify our best feature – before the axe falls.

Fianna Fáil Ard Fheis speech, March 2009

We're still waiting

"The Green Party is committed to real change and to achieve this, Fianna Fáil and the Progressive Democrats must be removed from government."

The Green Party's John Gormley talks about change we can't believe in. *The Sun*, 22 May 2007

Unlikely bedfellows

"We are lying there bollix naked next to Fianna Fáil."

Maybe there was drink taken! Green Party TD Paul Gogarty gets disturbingly graphic about his party's relationship with Fianna Fáil. *Hot Press* interview, February 2009

The green planet

"[Eamon] was talking about saving the planet, but I'm not sure what planet he's speaking from."

Labour's Joan Burton worries about where Green Minister Eamon Ryan is coming from – literally! *Irish Independent*, 8 June 2009

Improved liquidity

"We are in unprecedented water."

Apparently it's much nicer than sparkling water. Taoiseach Brian Cowen addressing the IMI national leadership forum.

April 2009

Foggy forecast

"God, you know, I can't remember. I think it's 2.5%. I can't remember so I'm not going to . . ."

Tánaiste Mary Coughlan stands firm when asked about a Bank of Ireland report about economic forecasts.

The Sunday Times, 1 March 2009

I haven't the foggiest

"Bank of Ireland is more than entitled to put out their forecasts . . . we are working on what's been set down by the Department of Finance."

The Tánaiste was then reminded that Bank of Ireland was forecasting 7%–8%. Unfortunately for Mary Coughlan the Department of Finance was predicting a rate of 5.8%. Safe hands indeed! *The Sunday Times*, 1 March 2009

Action man

"An action has taken place that goes beyond the realms of fraud and is an action that is nothing less than economic treason."

Green Senator Dan Boyle resorts to hyperbole as he condemns the irregular accounting practices of Irish bankers.   *Sunday Tribune*, 15 February 2009

Dempsey's din

"There's no parallel in history for the damage that has been done except perhaps Cromwell – and even Cromwell was motivated by reasons other than personal gain!"

Not to be outdone, Transport Minister Noel Dempsey dusts off the history books to find some villainous parallels.

Fianna Fáil Ard Fheis speech, March 2009

Crucifixion scene

"Not since Pontius Pilate has anyone washed their hands so thoroughly of a report."

The villains just keep getting worse! Labour's Joan Burton castigating Brian Lenihan for his reaction to the IMF report on the Irish economy.   *RTE News*, 25 June 2009

Focus pocus

"I did not read the entirety of the report, because I focused on the risk factors outlined in the report."

Finance Minister Brian Lenihan's creative excuse in the Dáil for not reading the vital Anglo Irish Bank report.

Irish Independent, 12 February 2009

Assisted learning

"I did read extensive parts of the report which my officials outlined to me were of fundamental importance."

Aren't officials great! After that initial gaffe Brian Lenihan reassures us that he has people to do tiresome things like reading for him! *Irish Independent*, 12 February 2009

He needs it!

"He is getting his night's sleep, which he has done very well for the last couple of weeks ... and he's not taking a drink."

Mary O'Rourke – Brian Lenihan's aunt – doing the embarrassing auntie routine to perfection.

Irish Independent, 8 April 2009

Voting irregularity

"You haven't come of age, you've one year to go, of course. In Ireland you can only vote at 21, so you only have the right to protest and scream comprehensively at the age of 21."

Finance Minister Brian Lenihan has a talent for reassurance. The voting age in Ireland is eighteen.

The Sunday Times, 13 July 2008

We'll be grand!

"Regardless of what is happening internationally, there is no danger of a run on Irish banks."

Brian Lenihan again in September 2008 . . . The Finance Minister gets others to read his reports and is hazy on the voting age. Who wouldn't trust this man's assurances!

20 September 2008

Not a bother!

"The Government is confident about the strength and resilience of the Irish financial system."

Finance Minister Brian Lenihan on 20 September 2008 when the government increased the threshold for deposit protection insurance from €20,000 to €100,000.

"What we must do now is create an economy that combines the features of an attractive home for innovative multinationals while also being a highly attractive incubation environment for entrepreneurs."

Brian Cowen

We're saved! I think!

"What we must do now is create an economy that combines the features of an attractive home for innovative multinationals while also being a highly attractive incubation environment for entrepreneurs."

Taoiseach Brian Cowen saves the day with his clear, concise vision for the future . . . ahem . . .

The Irish Times, 22 November 2008

The wizard of odd

"Deputy Kenny has suggested the economy is going down the toilet in toto."

Brian Cowen drags Dorothy's dog from *The Wizard of Oz* into the economic blame game.

Sunday Independent, 13 June 2009

An Offaly big hole

"All of the local issues that would normally arise in a local election contest, ranging from bush-cutting to potholes . . . have been blown off the map in terms of the economic situation. Brian Cowen has created the biggest pothole of all and he's in it himself."

Enda Kenny digs deep and eventually tracks down the Taoiseach.

Size isn't everything!

"People need to understand that Europe is not about crooked bananas and the size of sausage rolls. Europe is fundamental to how this country can cope in the future."

So where do we go for justice if our sausage rolls are too small? Taoiseach Brian Cowen speaking on RTÉ's *Marian Finucane Show.*   8 February 2009

Backward step

". . .Taking some steps back so we can go forward again."

Taoiseach Brian Cowen speaking at a press conference – or was it a line dancing lesson?   3 February 2009

Siege mentalist!

"The opposition parties' . . . unfounded claims have been picked up abroad . . . Loose talk costs jobs!"

Taoiseach Brian Cowen decides to point the finger of blame at the opposition – for telling the truth. Shame on them!
                    The Donegal Democrat, 4 June 2009

Credit crunchers

"Recessions are tough. They hurt people . . ."

Brian Cowen should bring in the Gardaí to track down these menacing recessions!   Fianna Fáil Ard Fheis speech, March 2009

Parish preach

"We're a beautifully complex people. A nation of a thousand parishes . . ."

Brian Cowen waxes lyrical at the Fianna Fáil Ard Fheis.

March 2009

Mind games

"To make a dawn for the day again we must stick together. Ireland holds us all together and we must mind her now."

Brian Cowen needs a bit of minding himself after this poetic flourish at the Fianna Fáil Ard Fheis.   March 2009

Throwing us a lifeline

"It's time for pulling together."

Taoiseach Brian Cowen inspires us all at the Fianna Fáil Ard Fheis.

March 2009

No we can't!

"Those increasingly tiresome invocations of Barack Obama didn't help either. This isn't America. Brian Cowen is not the US president. Get over it."

Miriam Lord listening to Brian Cowen's Ard Fheis speech.

The Irish Times, 7 March 2009

Hearing loss

"I haven't heard any critical voices from anyone."

The Taoiseach Brian Cowen gives himself ten out of ten and rejects any suggestions of a backbench revolt.

The Mirror, 8 June 2009

Party pooper

"There is a lot of discontent in the party at the moment."

Ex-Junior Minister John McGuinness is obviously outside the Taoiseach's range of hearing.

The Late Late Show, RTÉ, 24 May 2009

Sinking ship

"We are like a boat in a very rough sea and it is important that we set our course in a sensible way to ensure we survive the storm."

Finance Minister Brian Lenihan sets sail into stormy budgetary waters.   *Metro*, 15 October 2008

Watertight analogies

"Ireland had a very exposed economy and had been hit first by the international financial tsunami . . ."

Brian Lenihan can't help wading in with some nautical analogies to describe our financial plight. Maybe he's trying to improve liquidity.   *The Irish Times*, 27 April 2009

Water retention

"The handling of this issue confirms, once again, that the government is all at sea on economic policy and is lurching from one U-turn to the next."

Fine Gael's Richard Bruton criticises the government's handling of the Anglo Irish Bank crisis. He's got a point about the government being at sea. They spend enough time talking about matters maritime.

Sunday Tribune, 18 January 2009

Water on the Brian

"It is not generally appreciated how far the banks had departed from their moorings."

Salty sea dog Minister Brian Lenihan is getting out of his depth at this stage. *The Belfast Telegraph*, 12 January 2009

Water, water everywhere

"We swim together or we sink together. We need Asia, China and India to be on board. The eye of the storm was in the US, but it is a global storm."

EU President José Manuel Barroso dips his toe into the ocean of maritime musings.

Sunday Tribune, 26 October 2008

Water pretension

"The Minister wants to pretend that this is some sort of an international tsunami."

Another wave of attack from Richard Bruton as he criticises Finance Minister Brian Lenihan.

RTÉ News at One, 25 June 2009

Hot air

"We are exposed to the harsh winds that are blowing in the Anglo-American world at present."

Finance Minister Brian Lenihan harnesses wind power to absolve himself of blame for the credit crunch.

The Irish Times, 13 June 2008

On shaky ground

"We've got to now revisit all of those issues because of the seismic earthquake that has taken place."

Taoiseach Brian Cowen opts for more earth-shattering imagery to explain our economic woes!

RTÉ News at One, 26 June 2009

Weather beaten

"We have faced into an economic tsunami!"

Maybe it's Met Éireann we need to solve our problems! Taoiseach Brian Cowen opts for a more familiar analogy.

RTÉ News at One, 26 June 2009

A vow of silence, Tánaiste?

"I really would love if we found ourselves in the situation where we won't talk ourselves into an even bigger crisis than we presently are in."

Talkative Tánaiste Mary Coughlan.

Morning Ireland, RTÉ, 25 February 2009

Sound judgement!

"The fundamentals of the Irish banking system were sound. No issues have been raised by the Central Bank or the Department of Finance at Government level about the banking system."

A good example of talking yourself into a bigger crisis. Tánaiste Mary Coughlan gives her considered opinion on the state of Irish banks – weeks before the government had to bail out the banks with the guarantee scheme.

The Daily Mail, 19 September 2008

Hasn't a clue!

*"You couldn't even discuss the exchequer figures yesterday,
you were so unknowledgeable."*

Joan Burton to Mary Coughlan in the Dáil.

Sunday Tribune, 8 March 2009

Contrary Mary

"You just watch it now."

Mary Coughlan's considered reply to Joan Burton.

Sunday Tribune, 8 March 2009

And totally wrong!

"Fiscally sustainable, economically appropriate and politically responsible."

Then Minister for Finance Brian Cowen commenting on his book of estimates in 2006 – loosely translated as wrong, wrong and wrong again!   19 November 2006

Driving us round the bend

"A measured deceleration is required, not a sudden slamming of brakes . . ."

Then Finance Minister Brian Cowen's budget day speech in 2007 on his long-term Government spending plans.

You don't say!

"With the benefit of hindsight it is clear that more should have been done to contain the housing market."

Finance Minister Brian Lenihan is certainly one of the best and brightest!   *The Mirror*, 8 April 2009

There's an iceberg!

"While the economy has performed well in the year so far the indications are that the short to medium term outlook has deteriorated somewhat."

Then Finance Minister Brian Cowen has his finger on the pulse.   5 October 2007

It's just some ice, really!

"We must not lose sight of the fact that the fundamentals of the economy are still good."

Brian Cowen reminds us that there's nothing to worry about, while still Finance Minister.   6 December 2007

Oh it's an iceberg all right . . .

"We are in a new era, never faced by anybody of our generation before. This is the worst financial crisis to hit the world since 1929."

Well, we all make mistakes! Even Taoiseach Brian Cowen.
                                        The Irish Times, 7 March 2009

Snouts in the trough

"I welcome that action against people who've used the Irish economy as their own personal piggy-bank."

It must be a big piggy-bank – hopefully they can find the key. Noel Dempsey speech at the Fianna Fáil Ard Fheis.

March 2009

Unnatural birth

"The Government has wasted valuable time, money and political capital on a tortuous talks process that was akin to a lengthy labour that produced a mouse."

Fine Gael's Richard Bruton may know lots about economics but he may need a refresher course in the birds and the bees. *Sunday Tribune*, 8 February 2009

Holey unacceptable

"We cannot continue to pour money into a bucket which is leaking this fast, when there is no prospect of repair."

If it's about the Irish banking crisis, then no politician – even Fine Gael's Richard Bruton – can resist an aquatic analogy! Here he's talking about Anglo Irish Bank losing €3.8 billion in six months. *The Associated Press*, 29 May 2009

Either would be nice!

"There is a world of difference between a solvent bank and a bank that is thriving."

Finance Minister Brian Lenihan obviously hasn't heard of the expression "beggars can't be choosers".

The London Times, 24 November 2008

Please sir, can we have more . . . bank guarantees?

"People are complaining that only six banks are covered. The six in question would have been orphans . . . if the . . . Irish State had not supported them."

Finance Minister Brian Lenihan, the Mother Teresa of banjaxed banks.   *The Sunday Tribune*, 5 October 2008

Cosy relationship

"An extra cocoon of Lenihan insulation from the cold winds of the market for our wretched banks."

Labour Finance spokesperson Joan Burton's multi-layered criticism of Brian Lenihan's move to extend the bank guarantee scheme beyond 2010.

The Irish Times, 24 June 2009

I predict a riot

"I can see great potential for arguments down the courts if we don't get it right and even if we do get it right ..."

National Treasury Management Agency boss Michael Somers hedges his bets!　　*The Sunday Times*, 14 June 2009

Behind closed doors

"We are trying to bolt a stable door clearly after the horse has gone a bit unruly."

Finance Minister Brian Lenihan just can't resist messing with a perfectly good cliché.　　*Irish Independent*, 27 February 2009

Oh, it's our fault now?

"I am saying to people: we are living beyond our means."

Brian Lenihan spreads the blame too widely. What's this "we" stuff, paleface?　　*Morning Ireland*, RTÉ, 3 December 2008

Could be worse!

"It's possible that places like Zimbabwe have bigger contractions. But you know when you're in trouble when you're saying at least we're not Zimbabwe."

Economist Alan Barrett of the ESRI looks for the silver lining
– I think!   *The Guardian*, 30 May 2009

Stable fable

"In terms of monetary and banking stability, we are in a very good position."

As compared to Zimbabwe again, perhaps? Finance Minister Brian Lenihan.   *The Irish Times*, 13 June 2008

Financial wizard!

"Looking back, it would appear that economic success had fostered a false sense of invincibility."

Finance Minister Brian Lenihan continues to dazzle us with his conclusions about the causes of the credit crunch.

PA Newswire, 7 April 2009

Out of sight, out of mind

"To identify the problem that is there and park it somewhere else so we can deal with it over a longer period."

Brian Cowen talking about kicking to touch, sorry, solving the problems in the banking sector.

IMI leadership forum, April 2009

I just don't know!

"There are those who don't know and there are those who don't know that they don't know."

Richard Bruton reacting to the IMF report on the Irish economy.   *RTÉ News*, 25 June 2009

The George cross

"A filthy transaction . . . it's an absolute outrage . . . a fraudulent presentation."

And this was before George Lee left RTÉ! The former economics editor gets upset about the Anglo Irish Bank deal with Irish Life and Permanent.   14 February 2009

Dances with wounded economies

"Fine Gael and the Labour party will one day regret the way they danced around our wounded economy."

Noel Dempsey may have a future as a *Dancing On Ice* judge. He certainly was on a roll at the Fianna Fáil Ard Fheis.

March 2009

"He's a great wit, mad about football, greyhounds."

Christy Cowen on his brother Brian

Gone to the dogs

"He's a great wit, mad about football, greyhounds."

At least he's got some talents. Christy Cowen on his brother Brian.   *Irish Examiner*, 5 July 2008

FF. . .ing language

"Ring those people and get a handle on it, will you bring in all those fuckers."

Taoiseach Brian Cowen whispers sweet nothings to Mary Coughlan in the Dáil. He's quite the charmer!

Irish Independent, 10 January 2009

Bank withdrawals

"It is a violent word but there should be a cull of executives in the banking system."

Green Party Senator Dan Boyle's version of bad language!

The Irish Times, 20 December 2008

Food critic

"We are faced with the prospect of a chalk and cheese coalition."

Environment Minister John Gormley is worried about alternative governments. Are Fianna Fáil and the Greens a steak and salad combo?   *The Irish Times*, 10 June 2009

Green eggs and ham

"We are faced with an opposition who believes you can make an omelette without cracking an egg."

We discover that John Gormley likes to start sentences with "we are faced" and is worried about the opposition's culinary skills.   *The Irish Times*, 10 June 2009

Dole Éireann

"I'm never resigned to joblessness or unemployment."

Finance Minister Brian Lenihan's head-scratching sentence construction! He may have to resign himself to joblessness soon.   *Morning Ireland*, RTÉ, 25 June 2009

Not my Dan Brown paperbacks!

"It is now time that the Government put away their golf clubs, suntan lotion and Dan Brown paperbacks and got a grip on the deteriorating Irish economy."

At least the Government are prepared for any extra leisure time they get in the future. Fine Gael Finance spokesman Richard Bruton's rallying call after the Dáil's rather long summer recess.   *The Irish Times*, 5 September 2008

Hopelessly Optimistic Crunchies

The People Who (Unfortunately) Always Look on the Bright Side

Off his booming rocker!

"There's no recession. It's a pre-boom."

Damian Ryan, manager of Dublin pub Doheny & Nesbitt, makes his comments as customers switch from spirits to pints to make their drinks last longer.

The Irish Times, 6 March 2009

Buffet service

"A simple rule dictates my buying: Be fearful when others are greedy, and be greedy when others are fearful. And most certainly, fear is now widespread . . ."

Famed American investor Warren Buffett. He coins the phrase of the year by urging us to be greedy when others are fearful – or is it the other way round?

The New York Times, October 2008

Blood bank

"Buy when there's blood in the streets, even if the blood is your own."

Quote attributed to eighteenth-century British banker Lord Rothschild.

Fundamental flaw

"The fundamentals of our economy are sound."

US presidential election candidate John McCain giving the US economy two thumbs up on Monday, 15 September 2008. The same day, 158-year-old Wall Street firm Lehman Brothers filed for bankruptcy and 94-year-old Merrill Lynch sold itself to Bank of America.

Anglo Irish plank

"Our exposure is not to the building, it's to the money that comes from the leasing of it . . . if the value of the property goes down, it doesn't matter. We still get our loan repaid."

Anglo Irish Bank chairman Sean Fitzpatrick speaking at his company's AGM in February 2008. Since then the bank has been nationalised, with the Government planning an injection of up to €4 billion. Anglo also reported pre-tax losses of €4.1 billion in the six months to March 2009 – and Sean Fitzpatrick resigned over secret loans in late 2008.

Shocking complacency

"Not only have individual financial institutions become less vulnerable to shocks from underlying risk factors, but also the financial system as a whole has become more resilient."

Former Federal Reserve Chairman Alan Greenspan speaking in 2004. He should have got a second opinion!

Quoted in *The New York Times*, 9 October 2008

Another shocker!

"Irish banks are resilient and have good shock absorption capacity."

Former Irish Financial Regulator Patrick Neary. He's obviously a fan of Alan Greenspan's speeches.

The Irish Times, 19 September 2008

This will end in tears

"We've been seeing stress and strains . . . but this is against the backdrop of a strong global economy."

The stresses and strains were fund rescues, bankruptcy filings, near collapses in the previous two weeks. You have to hand it to former US Treasury Secretary Henry Paulson – he was an optimist. *The Irish Times*, 24 August 2007

Don't mention the "R" word

"I don't want to use the word recession."

The Economic and Social Research Institute's Alan Barrett is careful not to talk down the outlook for the economy. Hell, you should have used the "R" word, Alan! It would have prepared us.   *The Irish Times*, 6 July 2007

No they weren't!

"Pessimistic predictions ... of a collapse [of the housing market] from the International Monetary Fund [IMF] and The Economist magazine are, at best, unwarranted and based on inappropriate models and, at worst, they are sensationalist."

Economist Dr Maurice Roche in a report for the Economic and Social Research Institute criticises *The Economist* magazine for saying the Irish housing bubble would soon burst. ESRI – maybe it means Everything Should Right Itself?   19 December 2003

Envy's the wrong word

"[This] country's system of housing finance is the envy of the world."

American Treasury Secretary John Snow made these comments while appealing to the US Congress not to impose tighter controls on the Fannie Mae and Freddie Mac lending institutions.   *The Economist*, 18 October 2003

Who really wants to be a millionaire?

"If only I'd listened to CNBC, I'd have $1 million today – provided I had started with $100 million."

The US comedian Jon Stewart, the presenter of *The Daily Show*, lampooning the business network through a video montage of bad stock market predictions made by CNBC analysts.

Capital dunce

"There are no plans for any inorganic capital raisings of any sort . . . The capital ratios are there. If you want to go and make up your own, feel free."

Sir Fred Goodwin (now former) CEO of British bank Royal Bank of Scotland, scoffing at the thought, in February 2008, that his bank would need more capital. In less than two months, the bank needed a record £12 billion rights issue.

Quoted in *The Independent,* 1 January 2009

Faraway hills are greener

"I am seeing a few green shoots but it's a little bit too early to say exactly how they'd grow."

The day that 4,000 British job losses were announced, British Government Minister Baroness Vadera began predicting the end of the recession. *The Sun*, 15 January 2009

Put a sack in it, Bishop!

"Sometimes people seem to be relieved to get off the treadmill. In some circumstances it's good to get the sack."

Richard Chartres, the Bishop of London. It's easy to say that when you've a job for life – and possible eternal life to look forward to, Right Reverend!

The Sunday Times, 15 February 2009

We're not there yet . . . but we're getting there

"I think that we are getting closer to the end of the financial crisis. It is not fully over yet, but the signs from the United States are encouraging."

Josef Ackermann, the CEO of Deutsche Bank, sees light at the end of the tunnel, while the rest of us just saw the oncoming train!

Reuters UK, 19 May 2008

Bad Call!

"He is very, very good at calling the US equity market. This guy has managed to return 1 to 1.2 per cent per month, year after year after year."

UK investor nicknamed Superwoman Nicola Horlick. Her firm Bramdean Asset Management had $21 million invested with Bernie Madoff. Oops!   *The Independent*, 13 December 2008

Bottoms up!

"We continue to expect economic activity to bottom out, then to turn up later this year."

Ben Bernanke, the Chairman of the US Federal Reserve, lays it on the line with an optimistic forecast. Let's hope he's right!   *The Daily Telegraph*, 6 May 2009

Path of destruction

"A lot can still go wrong, but at least I can see a path that will bring us out of this entire episode relatively intact."

But he's been wrong before! Ben Bernanke in August 2008 speaking about the recovery of the American economy . . . he was wrong!   Quoted in *The New Yorker*, 1 December 2008

You're fired!

"Today we announced a number of strategic measures to reflect the continuing evolution of the financial markets over the past year."

This is an email extract from Brady Dougan, the Credit Suisse CEO – which actually calls for 5,300 redundancies at the bank.

They're bankers!

"There is an exposure in the Irish banks, but they made it clear they can accommodate it. The analysts of the different firms that look at bank shares and bank performances have said the Irish banks can weather this crisis."

Minister for Finance Brian Lenihan wasn't checking the roof while the sun was shining with a weather forecast like that!

Evening Herald, 11 October 2008

Gloom with a view

"A similar rate of growth is expected in 2007 [5.5%], despite an expected downturn in the global economy. Furthermore the outlook beyond 2007 may not be as gloomy as often predicted."

A 2006 Allied Irish Bank economic report. Memo to the AIB economic unit: err on the side of gloom in future!

The Daily Mail, 29 August 2006

I was brilliant!

"When I was Finance Minister in 2006 and 2007, the Ireland country reports [of the IMF] commended our economic management and sound fiscal position . . ."

Taoiseach Brian Cowen putting the best spin possible on his tenure as Finance Minister – following the 2009 IMF report that criticised decisions made while he was Minister.

The Irish Times, 4 July 2009

What the IMF really said in 2007

"Risks to the short term outlook . . . are tilted to the downside . . . if realised these risks would further dampen economic growth, reduce government revenue and increase financial sector stress . . . the risk of a sharper slowdown remains."

The International Monetary Fund report for 2007 wasn't quite as optimistic as Brian Cowen lets on.

The Irish Times, 26 September 2007

What the IMF really said in 2006

"At this point, concerns centre on the United States although other markets, such as those in Ireland, Spain and the UK, still seem overvalued by most conventional measures."

The International Monetary Fund raises the spectre of a property crash.   *The Irish Times*, 16 September 2006

Oh, and this as well in 2006

"Sunny in the short term, but there are clouds on the horizon."

The International Monetary Fund issuing a forecast for the Irish economy.   *The Irish Times*, 12 August 2006

It's bad to talk

"For anybody to be even uttering that in the present circumstances with the strength of the economy, they are being misguided to say the least."

Former Australian Prime Minister John Howard rejects talk of recession back in 2006. In early 2009, Australia only avoided a technical recession thanks to a government stimulus package and interest rate cuts.

Forbes.com, 8 March 2006

Half full of it!

"Construction is hugely strong at present and looks as if it will be for the medium term. I'm always sceptical of the glass half-empty."

Then Taoiseach Bertie Ahern speaking at the Irish Management Institute's annual management conference in Wicklow back in 2006. He really was keeping his hand on the tiller towards the end! *The Irish Times*, 8 April 2006

Soft in the head

"The consensus scenario for the housing market is a soft landing..."

Then Tánaiste Mary Harney rubbishes reports that the construction sector is in trouble.   *The Irish Times*, 8 August 2006

Wrong!

"Really we should have an examination into why so many people got it so wrong. My view is there's not a great problem. Really, the bad advice of last year given by so many has maybe made some people make mistakes, that they should have bought last year."

Then Taoiseach Bertie Ahern backs the builders back in 2006 and shoots the messengers warning about the property bubble.   *Sunday Tribune*, 7 May 2006

Not going to happen!

"To get a sustained fall in prices there must be some form of demand shock. This could occur through a major increase in interest rates or a substantial increase in unemployment, neither of which was very likely in the current environment."

Dan McLaughlin, Bank of Ireland chief economist, reacts to *The Economist* magazine's report on Ireland and other countries with overheated property markets.

The Irish Times, 31 May 2003

At least he's consistent!

"This is unlikely to precipitate a serious correction in borrowing or house prices, but may well dampen mortgage growth to some degree."

Bank of Ireland economist Dan McLaughlin speaking about the likely effect of European interest rates rising by 1% by the end of 2006.   *Irish Independent*, 22 November 2005

Spot on!

"Despite all the doom and gloom warnings by the Central Bank and The Economist *magazine . . . there is no sign of the Irish property 'bubble' bursting any time soon, according to the results of a property survey by Ken O'Brien's specialist monthly journal* Finance. *The survey, based on the views of a panel of leading economists, predicts an average growth of 4.6% per annum over the next five years – at a rate of 9% this year (2004), followed by four years of more moderate growth."*

An article from *The Irish Times* residential property supplement,

10 June 2004

It gets worse!

". . . Niall O'Grady of Permanent TSB foresees an average growth of 7.8% per annum over the next five years; however, his forecast relies on the rental market remaining strong – where have you been Niall? – and the stock market remaining weak, making the property sector a more attractive investment."

The same *Irish Times* article.

What's wrong with you, man?

"The pessimist of the bunch is Alan McQuaid of Bloxham Stockbrokers, who predicts an average growth of just 1.7% over the next five years – 5.6% this year falling to –0.2% in 2007."

Again the same *Irish Times* residential property supplement.

10 June 2004

In the meantime, there's always bicycle hire schemes and bacon sandwiches."

Boris Johnson

Pig in a spoke

"Some day, this recession is going to end. Confidence is going to come surging back with all the biological inevitability of the new infatuation that follows a broken heart. In the meantime, there's always bicycle hire schemes and bacon sandwiches."

The Mayor of London Boris Johnson tries to give us a bit of a lift in these gloomy times. Using love as an analogy makes a change from green shoots.   *The Irish Times*, 19 December 2008

I love the smell of recession in the morning!

"I want to quote Colonel Kilgore in Apocalypse Now *when he says, 'Someday, captain, this war is going to end.'"*

London Mayor Boris Johnson again. What is he on? He is truly out of step with the times with these rousing comments!   *The Mail on Sunday*, 4 February 2009

Super Gordon

"We not only saved the world ..."

British Prime Minister Gordon Brown gives himself superhero status, albeit because of a slip of the tongue.
                                      The Times, 10 December 2008

Contrite Crunchies

Why Nobody Says Sorry

Back seat drivers . . . grrr!

"People say I caused it now, don't they? Well, that's wrong. To be honest with you, it never would have happened, but that's another day's work."

Bertie Ahern. Oh, if only I was in charge!

The Sunday Business Post, 31 August 2008

You're history

"Some people are trying to re-write history and are blaming me, Brian Cowen, Charlie McCreevy and Ray MacSharry for the current position, but this sort of talk is nonsense."

Bertie Ahern clearly thinks we're all deluded. Well, we did elect his Government three times, I suppose.

I'm f***ing sorry, okay?

"It wasn't appropriate whether it's inside or outside the Dáil. I apologise for it. I put my hand up. I think it's the manly thing to do."

He's a real man! Brian Cowen won't apologise for overheating the economy but will say sorry for using bad language! Here he's apologising for using the "f"-word in the Dáil.   *Irish Independent*, 23 May 2008

Delirium tremors

"We find a hard landing for that [housing market] because of the seismic shock that's taken place."

Taoiseach Brian Cowen speaking about the property market crash. It's clear the government have nothing to apologise for. Instead the Met Office should get the blame for not forecasting those seismic shocks. *RTÉ News at One*, 26 June 2009

Word games

"This is the old apology . . . word game that you've been engaging here for some months . . . you're not asking opposition people to come in here and apologise for the fact that they're asking to spend more."

Maybe because they're not in power? Taoiseach Brian Cowen gets apoplectic about apologising with interviewer Sean O'Rourke.   *RTÉ News at One*, 26 June 2009

Above and beyond

"Some of those who were looking for an apology from me were asking me to do even more."

Maybe they actually want you to mean it when you say sorry. Brian Cowen clearly has apology issues!

RTÉ News at One, 26 June 2009

His number one fan

"I've said I've got more right than I get wrong!"

Taoiseach Brian Cowen denies he's ever refused to apologise. But I don't think this statement clears things up.

RTÉ News at One, 26 June 2009

Fianna fool

"Of course I don't claim I got everything right in my political career, only a fool would suggest that."

But you don't claim you got anything wrong either, Mr Cowen.

The Star, 20 May 2009

It wasn't my fault!

"What is it that you think I should be apologising for? I have nothing to apologise for. You guys just don't get it, do you?"

British Prime Minister Gordon Brown speaking to reporters about the possibility of apologising for his involvement in the credit crunch.   *The Independent*, 17 March 2009

Exporting problems

"I take full responsibility for all my actions. Perhaps ten years ago after the Asian crisis we should have been forcing these issues on to the agenda . . . But we're dealing with a problem that is global."

Gordon Brown again. Has he been taking advice from Brian Cowen on this apology lark? Remember, everyone, the problem is global – i.e. not my fault.   *The Mirror*, 17 March 2009

Gordon the plasterer

"He thinks . . . that Britain is just the innocent victim of a banking crisis that 'came from America', and that all we need to do is apply a few sticking plasters to an otherwise healthy body."

Tory leader David Cameron speaking about Gordon Brown's strategy of blaming external events for Britain's troubles.
                                        ITN, 14 March 2009

You'll be waiting, Horst!

"I still haven't heard a clearly audible mea culpa."

German president Horst Kohler on the fact that nobody from the banks has said sorry for the part they played in the global financial crisis.

Bus pass

"Blaming hedge funds is like blaming the passengers on a bus crash."

Hedge fund trader Paul Marshall hops on the heavily oversubscribed "it's not my fault" bus.

The Sunday Times, 1 February 2009

From minted to tormented

"I'm sorry . . . I live in a tormented state now, knowing of the pain and suffering that I've created."

US fraudster Bernie Madoff says sorry after receiving a 150-year sentence for masterminding a massive fraud that robbed investors of $65 billion. He kind of needed to apologise, don't you think? *The Los Angeles Times*, 30 June 2009

Don't mention it

"I can't say sorry with any degree of sincerity and decency, but I do say thank you."

Anglo Irish Bank chairman Sean Fitzpatrick charms the nation by thanking the Irish taxpayer for the bank guarantee scheme.

The Marian Finucane Show, RTÉ, 4 October 2008

Sorry excuse

"It is clear to me, on reflection, that it was inappropriate and unacceptable from a transparency point of view."

Anglo chairman Sean Fitzpatrick's resignation statement two months later. For resigning, Sean, we say, "thank you"!

The Sunday Business Post, 28 December 2008

Sorry mess

"I apologise on behalf of myself and the board. I am really sorry that this has happened."

Well, Seanie wouldn't apologise so somebody had to. Donal O'Connor, the new chairman of Anglo Irish Bank, after Sean Fitzpatrick's unauthorised loans were revealed.

Press Association, 16 January 2009

Regrets . . . I've not had a few!

"I'm not sure if it comes to an apology as such. I do regret some of our decisions. I have to balance that with lots and lots of good decisions that we made."

Five letters beginning with "s"? Rhymes with "lorry"? Any takers? Not Bank of Ireland CEO Brian Goggin. He nearly apologises but then thinks better of it.

RTÉ News, 12 February 2009

Human dynamo

"We are used to a less dynamic environment than we have seen in the past few months and days."

Chairman of British bank Bradford and Bingley, Rod Kent. Rod's effort is a unique take on an apology. It was all too hectic for me! Quoted in *The Independent*, 1 January 2009

For God's sake, apologise

"There are some huge moral lessons to be learnt about the nature of accumulating wealth . . . A lot of people are waiting to hear an acknowledgement of some responsibility for irresponsible behaviour."

Archbishop Rowan Williams will be waiting! Even men of the cloth are getting fed up of the pinstriped brigade's inability to say sorry. *Sydney Morning Herald*, 26 December 2008

Yes, you have!

"They must be divorced, the global liquidity situation and the rumours and speculation about property in Ireland. We have made mistakes and I'll admit that. Have we been reckless? No, we haven't."

Sean Fitzpatrick continues to convince us that everything is okay.   *The Marian Finucane Show*, RTÉ, 4 October 2008

Regrettable

"I suppose if I have a regret it is that I didn't see this coming."

Bank of Ireland chief executive Brian Goggin shouldn't bank on the sympathy vote with comments like that.
                              RTÉ interview, 12 February 2009

Strong apology

"CEOs should realise that an apology is not a sign of weakness, but an act of strength."

That makes our government very lightweight indeed! Leslie Gaines-Ross, chief reputation strategist at public relations firm Weber Shandwick.   *USA Today*, 21 October 2008

Lending

"I've made mistakes in lending."

Richie Boucher, new CEO of Bank of Ireland, may be taking that advice.   *The Irish Times*, 19 May 2009

"Are there changes that I would contemplate were I to know now that we would be in this position? Of course, there'd be different decisions that you would take. But we don't all have crystal balls."

Brian Cowen

Crystal balls

"Are there changes that I would contemplate were I to know now that we would be in this position? Of course, there'd be different decisions that you would take. But we don't all have crystal balls."

Taoiseach Brian Cowen doesn't say sorry and instead bemoans his lack of the appropriate equipment.

The Irish Times, 30 March 2009

They made me do it!

"I take all the responsibility for all of the decisions that I have taken. They were taken by me on the basis of the best possible advice available to me at the time."

A bad workman always blames his tools! Taoiseach Brian Cowen puts the con into contrition by blaming his advisors.

The Irish Times, 30 March 2009

That's decent of you

"A lot of the time you get it right and you carry on. Some of the times you get it wrong, and you should say you got it wrong."

Transport Minister Noel Dempsey has it all figured out.

Sunday Independent, 15 March 2009

A Clinton apology!

"So I misspoke."

An apology – Hillary Clinton style – during the US Presidential election campaign.   24 March 2008

Tax discredit

"I should have been more careful. I take full responsibility for them."

US Treasury Secretary designate Timothy Geithner takes responsibility for underpaying his taxes by almost $50,000. Next stop apology?   *The Miami Herald*, 22 January 2009

Direct apology shocker!

"I screwed up."

US President Barack Obama leads the way by uttering an unequivocal apology after two of his cabinet nominations withdrew after tax irregularities.

Chicago Tribune, 29 April 2009

Self-examination

"I would have to say if I was to run that again, would I run it differently? The answer is yes."

Taoiseach Brian Cowen. When someone asks himself questions and then answers them himself, you know he's trying to get out of apologising.

The Late Late Show, RTÉ, September 2008

Questions and answers

"Is it right for the banks to take their share of the responsibility, is it right for the banks to apologise for . . . getting some big judgements wrong . . . is it right for us to acknowledge that? Absolutely it is."

UK bank Barclays chief executive John Varley also asks himself questions and then answers them. He's just not that into apologising, methinks! *AFP*, 14 January 2009

Looking after himself!

"A good long rest is the first order of priority."

This is what UK banker Sir Fred Goodwin said on leaving his CEO job with Royal Bank of Scotland. He also left with a pension pot worth £8 million sterling. The UK Government was forced to bail out the bank using £20 billion sterling of taxpayers' money. *The Times*, 10 February 2009

Lingering doubts

"You should be in no doubt about a degree of contrition."

Royal Bank of Scotland chairman Sir Tom McKillop after a record £12 billion rights issue. Somehow there are still doubts!   Quoted in *The Independent*, 1 January 2009

Now, doesn't that feel better?

"I am sorry about the very real financial and therefore human cost that those who have invested in us now feel . . . and I am also sorry if any of our customers have suffered anxiety as a result of the situation."

Sir Tom McKillop again. He's trying his best!
                    Quoted in *The Independent*, 1 January 2009

It's all about you . . .

"I could not be more sorry for what has happened. But I've invested a lot in RBS . . ."

Sir Fred Goodwin, former chief executive of British bank RBS . . . looking in vain for the sympathy vote.
                    The Financial Times, 11 February 2009

Mea not culpa

"I'm not personally culpable for the crisis."

UK banker Andy Hornby, the former CEO of HBOS (now merged with Lloyds) distances himself.

The Irish Times, 10 February 2009

Oh, poor you!

"We are profoundly, and I think I would say unreservedly sorry at the turn of events ... all of us have lost a great deal of money."

Lord Stevenson, former chairman of UK bank HBOS, is up for an apology – but only if we feel sorry for him first.

The Financial Times, 11 February 2009

I'm really reeeeeally sorry!

"Apologies from RBS and HBOS had a polished and practised air."

UK Treasury select committee report about the behaviour of HBOS and RBS bosses during the credit crunch.

The Daily Mail, 15 May 2009

Puntastic

"Scumbag millionaires"

The Sun's front-page headline after the four aforementioned bankers appeared before a House of Commons committee and attempted their apologies.   11 February 2009

Base point

"I'm not aware of any basis for questioning my integrity as a result of it all."

Sir Fred Goodwin's response when asked if he has a different moral compass to other people.

The Financial Times, 11 February 2009

Customers, schmustomers!

"There has been huge anxiety and uncertainty caused for our colleagues . . . but also, for periods of time, for our customers."

UK banker Lord Stevenson, the ex-HBOS chairman, spares a thought for the customers.　*The Guardian*, 10 February 2009

Up front!

"We boobed."

In 2009 Marks & Spencer added a £2 sterling premium to the price of big bras to increase revenue. This is the headline on the ad announcing that the surcharge was to go.

Cookie monsters

"You come here today on your bicycles after buying Girl Scout cookies and helping out Mother Teresa. You're saying, 'We're sorry. We didn't mean it. We won't do it again. Trust us.' I have some people in my [district] who have robbed some of your banks and they say the same thing."

Boston Republican Michael Capuano loses patience with the bankers at a US House of Representatives hearing.

The Associated Press, 11 February 2009

Not passing the buck

"I cannot find words to describe our disappointment, embarrassment and shock over the above results. I find management teams that blame disappointing performance on environmental factors rather than their own poor decisions quite frustrating – and in reviewing the above I recognise that I have just done that, and I apologise."

Now here's a guy that could teach the two Brians a thing or two. Investor Lee Ainslie III, the managing partner of Maverick, after an announcement of dipped profits.

The Sunday Times, 2 November 2008

105

Underfloor bleating

"The report doesn't suggest that governments uniquely bear responsibility for this. No opposition party put forward policies to underheat the economy."

Finance Minister Brian Lenihan always welcomes an opportunity not to apologise! Defending criticism of government in the IMF report.

Morning Ireland, RTÉ, 25 June 2009

Never met them in my life, honest!

"I wasn't a member of that government."

Brian Lenihan's response when asked to apologise for government policy between 2002 and 2007. He was the Minister of State for Children from 2002 and in 2005 the role was upgraded to allow him to attend cabinet meetings.

Morning Ireland, RTÉ, 25 June 2009

Missing the key word

"The key issue is not this blame game . . . the key issue is what we do here and now."

Brian Lenihan sidesteps another opportunity to apologise.

Morning Ireland, RTÉ, 25 June 2009

Hot topic

"We did overheat the economy, I have always accepted that and I made that clear in my last Budget speech."

Brian Lenihan, the Finance Minister. He's "accepting" things – Government-speak for "we screwed up".

The Irish Times, 25 June 2009

The usual suspects

"Our difficulties in the last six months stem from an international phenomenon which everybody in the country can see on their television screen every evening. It is a world economic crisis."

Finance Minister Brian Lenihan. How many times can this man wash his hands of our financial crisis?

Sunday Independent, 14 December 2008

That old chestnut

"If all our difficulties related to the recent construction boom in Ireland, I would not be before you this afternoon. We are the living witnesses to the most dramatic collapse in the world financial order since 1929."

Brian Lenihan is at it again . . .

The Examiner, 13 April 2009

Tell 'em nothing!

"Be conservative in what you say, don't say anything more than you need to and avoid speculating about the future as much as possible."

Anonymous quote from the head of communications at a FTSE 100 group, on the credit crunch approach to apologising. *USNews.com*, 14 October 2009

Sorry excuse

"No one wants to stick their head above the parapet or be the one identified with this scandal. Saying sorry can be a dangerous thing."

One top executive at a large UK financial services company quoted in FT.com. *USNEWS.com*, 14 October 2008

Ah, no harm done!

"I and others were mistaken early on in saying that the subprime crisis would be contained."

US Federal Reserve Chairman Ben Bernanke, November 2008.
Quoted in *oantalk.co.uk*

Where exactly are we?

"Wallowing in where we are is no good. I have to take responsibility for where we are, the Government has to take responsibility for where we are, and we'll take responsibility for where we are going, I've no problem doing that."

Transport Minister Noel Dempsey sounds pretty disoriented by it all. Hope he's not responsible for designing roads!

Sunday Independent, 15 March 2009

Trouble in a bubble

"The basic proposition at the time was I was not sure if there was a bubble . . . In retrospect I was wrong. Hindsight is 20–20."

Professor Brian Lucey apologises for forecasting that there was no property bubble. But at least he apologised!

The Irish Times, 30 June 2009

He said sorry!

"I regret the impact of those decisions on our shareholders, our customers, our staff and on everyone else affected ... and, on behalf of the bank, I apologise to you for the anxiety and distress that many of you have suffered."

Apologising is the new black now that banks are all in the red! Must have been the rotten egg thrown at AIB chairman Dermot Gleeson that prompted him to say enough is enough!   *The Irish Times*, 14 May 2009

Apolog-ice

"I bear my share of the responsibility for the decisions at the time and for those mistakes it is right to apologise."

A politician who apologised! Rejoice! Former Icelandic Prime Minister Geir Haarde finally mentions the "a" word in a speech to parliament.   *Agence France Presse*, 27 March 2009

Villainous Crunchies

The Guys we Love to Hate

Frenemies

"People really hate you. And they're starting to hate us because we've been hanging out with you."

US politician Barney Frank, chairman of the House of Congress Finance Committee, is seriously worried about his street cred because he's got to hang out with a crowd of bankers. *The Irish Times*, 6 February 2009

Bureaucratic nightmares!

"A lot of the bureaucrats here are not just stupid and corrupt, but stupid, corrupt and evil."

Now here's a person who's taking no prisoners – Indonesian entrepreneur Gita Wirjawanan.

Euromoney Magazine, October 2008

"I want to see . . . bank managers wrestle with lions in the O2 arena"

Matthew Parris

Fruitful exercise

"The low hanging fruit . . . Idiots whose parents paid for prep school, Yale, and then the Harvard MBA, was there for the taking. All of this only ended up making it easier for me to find people stupid enough to take the other side of my trades. God bless America."

Andrew Lahde managed a hedge fund which made an 866% return in 2007 by betting the US subprime market would collapse. This is what he said when he decided to quit the markets. I don't think they'll miss you, Andrew!

The Irish Times, 24 October 2008

Now that's entertainment

"I want to see hedge-fund managers tipped into cage fights with naked Gypsies; bank managers wrestle with lions in the O2 arena; failed regulators thrown to alligators in the Royal Docks; short sellers in pits of snakes . . ."

Matthew Parris writing in *The Times* about the financial market collapse.

He's not finished!

". . . and distinguished City economists try their luck with sharks. They've had their heyday, their bonuses, their Porsches, their fine wines and oafish ostentation – they've had their fun. Now for ours. To the guillotine!"

Matthew Parris, *The Times*

Room for criticism

"The $1.2 million reported in the press was for the renovation of my office, two conference rooms and a reception area. The expenses were incurred over a year ago in a very different environment."

Merill Lynch's CEO John Thain's memo to employees after his sudden departure. His interior designing works out a very pre-credit crunch figure of $300,000 per room.

Euromoney Magazine, February 2009

It's curtains for you!

"The list includes an $87,000 'area rug', $28,000 for curtains, a $68,000 credenza and the perfect finishing touch: a $1,400 wastebasket. This is what passes for corporate responsibility?"

Commentator Campbell Brown speaking about former Merill Lynch boss John Thain's redecorating spree as the company was firing employees.   *CNN.com*, 22 January 2009

Flushing away tax dollars

". . . the government should give more scrutiny to companies that have received taxpayer assistance then going out and renovating bathrooms or offices or in other ways not managing those dollars appropriately."

US President Barack Obama speaking about extravagance in Wall Street.   *Bloomberg.com*, 23 January 2009

Flexitime

"It's well known that I take a fair bit of time off during the year. But I think it's a fair return for the very long hours that I put in . . . and for the loneliness and pressure of continuing to over achieve."

Anglo Irish Bank boss Sean Fitzpatrick. There has to be a role for him as a pantomime baddie this Christmas!

Business and Finance, 2002

Well done, you!

"I've had no overt negative criticism at all about how much I'm paid. Strangely perhaps for Irish people most people have said well done."

Sean Fitzpatrick proves why the Irish people are known the world over a being a very tolerant race.

Business and Finance, 2002

Too many Keanes . . .

"Why does Roy Keane go that extra yard for the ball when David Beckham doesn't? They're both paid the same. It's internal. I think we've a lot of Roy Keanes with a very clear view of what they want to achieve . . . but they know that if they do, they'll be rewarded well. "

Sean Fitzpatrick, whose team seems to be top-heavy with midfielders.   *Business and Finance*, 2002

Greed is good

"One of my senior executives actually went out of his way to say to me that the more I earned, the more he earned and the happier we all are."

Sean Fitzpatrick does a Gordon Gekko impression.
Business and Finance, 2002

Change of tune

"The boardrooms of Irish banks will have to take account of the views of taxpayers like never before . . . ensure people are paid appropriately and not excessively."

Sean Fitzpatrick.   RTÉ, 3 October 2008

Brains trust

"There is definitely a problem with the way banks have been run."

American academic Professor Eugene Fama – all-round brain box and inventor of the efficient market hypothesis – really gets to the bottom of it all.

The Irish Times, 26 September 2008

Stop your s-whining!

"It couldn't come at a worse time for the travel industry. It had seemed like things were starting to recover. This will probably set that back a little."

US analyst Matthew Jacob bemoans his fate as swine flu hits.

Poor Gary!

"Because of the credit crunch, everyone is feeling poor – even me."

Gary Lineker.   *Press Association Newsfile*, 19 June 2009

"The Minister and the Taoiseach remind me of First World War generals. . . . They called for wave after wave of sacrifices, giving rise to a famous phrase: Lions led by donkeys. That is the perfect description of the plight of the Irish people."

Joan Burton

Mirror, mirror!

"I look at myself in the morning and I'm very proud of what I have done and so are my partners. Nobody knew anything about anything."

The chief fundraiser of the Fairfield Greenwich Fund, Andres Piedrahita. The fund faces fraud charges over its role in putting clients' money into Bernie Madoff's funds.

The Evening Standard, 2 April 2009

Out to lunch

"Some people have even started bringing their own lunch to work."

Blog from a City-based financial worker on the BBC website after the crunch hit . . . The "odd" phenomenon was titled BYOL (Bring Your Own Lunch).

Animal crackers

"The Minister and the Taoiseach remind me of First World War generals. . . . They called for wave after wave of sacrifices, giving rise to a famous phrase: Lions led by donkeys. That is the perfect description of the plight of the Irish people."

Labour Finance spokeswoman Joan Burton engages in trench warfare.   *PA Newswire*, 7 April 2009

Olive branch?

"The green shoots show some sign of withering on the vine."

Maybe we need Gerry Daly to encourage new growth, cut back the dead wood and sort out the financial crisis. Jeremy Batstone, head of research at Charles Stanley in London.

Morning Ireland, RTÉ, 26 June 2009

Backing the wrong horse

"Trying to predict medium-term trends in the currency market at the moment is virtually impossible. It's rather like picking the worst horse in the glue factory."

Jeremy Batstone of Charles Stanley again . . . he sounds like he hasn't had his triple espresso yet!

Morning Ireland, RTÉ, 26 June 2009

Celebrity Crunchies

**Because the Credit Crunch even
Affects Famous People!**

Dogs of war

*"Maybe because dogs don't have the financial problems that
humans do, they're not involved in wars as much."*

Ex-*Friends* actress Lisa Kudrow explains why there will never
be a canine credit crunch – except when your dog decides
to chew your credit card.

The Sunday Times, 8 February 2009

Financial strain

*"Money can be a burden. That's why I got stressed last year. I
had a massive house that I couldn't control or clean."*

Carly Zucker, girlfriend of Chelsea soccer player Joe Cole, on
I'm a Celebrity . . . Get Me Out of Here! See how stressed you
get without it, Carly!

Spend our way out

"I'm in Australia, I think it's important to help out, you know, the economy out here, everywhere in the world. And what's wrong with doing a little shopping? It's New Year's, I need a New Year's dress."

Paris Hilton single-handedly hopes to boost Australian consumer spending! *BreitBart.com*, New Year's Day, 2009

Harsh criticism

". . . Please don't tell me. It's really harshing my mellow."

Big Brother presenter Davina McCall doesn't want to hear negative opinions. *Scotland on Sunday*, 28 June 2009

Facial expressions

"I'm preferring to be a lot more natural these days. I've tried Botox, I've tried all."

Really? You'd never notice! Singer Kylie Minogue is trying to get in tune with the times. *Scotland on Sunday*, 5 April 2009

Kitchen sink drama

"People think you go home and be a celeb, sipping Laurent-Perrier and listening to classical music. You don't. You go home and wash some pants in the sink."

Channel 4's Gok Wan is even reining things in . . . but did he really have to get rid of his washing machine?   16 April 2009

Fashionably broke

"The recession was a gift to the management . . . because they could blame everything on that, but it was only partly responsible. Do you know that I haven't been paid for a year and a half? I'm owed one million two hundred thousand euros! . . . I am too angry to cry."

Fashion designer Christian Lacroix getting hot under his designer collar because his couture house was put into voluntary receivership with mounting losses of €10 million.

The Sunday Telegraph, 21 June 2009

Cut your cloth

"There just aren't enough beluga-eating, stunningly beautiful, moneyed women in the world to keep Christian Lacroix's fantasy alive."

The writer Alice Olins diagnoses the problem for the famous French fashion house after it went into voluntary receivership.

The Daily Mail, 31 May 2009

Cut!

"Everything is being downsized because of the recession. Next year I'll be starring in a movie called New Zealand."

Australia star Hugh Jackman is worried about the effects of the credit crunch.   *The Sunday Times*, 1 March 2009

Slightly bonkers

"There is no group of people on the planet more stupid than bankers. They should be called bonkers."

Neat play on words there from filmmaker and restaurant critic Michael Winner.   *Press Association Newsfile*, 19 June 2008

Easy for you to say!

"Calm down, dear, it's only a recession."

Michael Winner is at it again. This time he reassures us with this message on his T-shirt while he was holidaying in bargain-basement Barbados.

The Mail on Sunday, 28 December 2008

Home dis-improvement

"There's no need for home-improvement shows on C4 now. They should encourage us to turn our houses into the value they were before, to avoid negative equity ... 'Destroy Your Home, with C4' ..."

Comedian Stewart Lee on getting some good telly out of the credit crunch.   *The Daily Record*, 9 April 2009

Pulp fiction

"I think the credit crunch is a brilliant thing. We should all stop moaning and start celebrating. When times are tough it's an opportunity to start looking at life in a different way."

I thought Jarvis Cocker already looked at life a different way. Maybe he'll become a hedge fund trader then.

Press Association Newsfile, 11 May 2009

Courtney stops

"I need to stop texting so much and send messages online."

Who says celebs don't know how to economise? Courtney Love knows how to save the pennies!

The Observer, 9 December 2007

"Sean Connery withdrew his money from the Royal Bank of Scotland and the whole world fell apart."

Roger Moore

Investing in Bonds

"Sean Connery withdrew his money from the Royal Bank of Scotland and the whole world fell apart."

Roger Moore's take on the causes of the credit crunch – and a dig at his predecessor as 007. I knew it had something to do with bonds!   *The Observer*, 21 December 2008

James Brum!

"If the credit crunch hits the movie business, who knows – Bond in Birmingham?"

Daniel Craig at the London opening of the latest Bond film, *Quantum of Solace*. Can't see Bond getting to do any sexy beach scenes in Birmingham.

Roll with it

"It'll be all right for the likes of me obviously because I'm fabulously wealthy. No credit crunch for me."

Reported remark by Noel Gallagher of Oasis.

Belfast Telegraph, 10 October 2008

Unlucky Guy

"Even Madonna has had to get rid of one of her personal assistants – Guy Ritchie."

Comedian Sacha Baron Cohen on how the recession is hitting Madonna. Don't think Guy was too bothered about being laid off though!   *The Mail on Sunday*, 18 January 2009

Older is wisest

"The economy is so bad A-Rod is dating Madonna just to get the senior citizen's discount."

Jay Leno leaps on a rumour that New York Yankees' Alex Rodriguez is dating fifty-year-old Madonna.

The Globe and Mail, 29 December 2008

Recession bites

"It's like a fabulous love bite. I've been a conscious consumer for a while now."

Supermodel Elle Macpherson's attempts to get into the recessionary shopping spirit certainly stand out all right!

The Observer, 12 May 2009

Good question, Ma'am!

"If these things were so large, how come everyone missed them?"

The Queen actually comes up with a good question while visiting the London School of Economics and Political Science. The economists are still arguing over the answer!

The Mail on Sunday, 9 November 2008

Never say never

"I genuinely think a crash is phenomenally unlikely to happen. People who make property make money in all markets and in all countries."

Maybe *Property Ladder* presenter Sarah Beeny should also take a trip to the London School of Economics? She needs a crash course fast.

The Irish Times, 11 April 2008

More!

"Some people fear extravagance, others meanness. I just have a neurotic need for too much. Too much everything."

Celebrity TV chef Nigella Lawson. That's not the spirit!

Scotland on Sunday, 22 February 2009

Non-financial support

"Stop smoking, start wearing a bra and stop shopping."

Actress Cameron Diaz telling us her New Year resolutions. We can learn from Cameron. We could use her New Year's resolutions to kick-start the economy – by stopping it from overheating, giving it more supports and boosting consumer confidence! Done! *The Mail on Sunday*, 4 January 2009

Jumpy financial institutions

"I wouldn't say I was rich, but I wrote a cheque last week and the bank bounced."

Comedian Frank Carson can't resist some credit crunch quips.   *The Sunday Mail*, 30 November 2008

Tell us!

"Oh, if only people knew how frugal we are."

Republican Vice Presidential candidate Sarah Palin defends herself after news got out that $150,000 of Republican Party money was spent on clothes for her and her family during the election campaign.   *The Observer*, 26 October 2008

Take one silver spoon

"It ruins people not having to earn money."

Nigella Lawson and her hubby Charles Saatchi disagree on what to leave their kids. His estimated wealth is £100 million while Nigella has £15 million. I'd say they could be on the road to ruin!   *The Observer*, 3 February 2008

Because I'm worth it!

"I'm worth a thousand BBC journalists."

Jonathan Ross hosting the British Comedy Awards jokes about his £6 million salary and cutbacks at the BBC. He wouldn't say that now!   *The Observer*, 9 December 2007

Stimulus package

"I am helping the economy by doing a lot of shopping . . ."

Paris Hilton again, boosting the fundamentals by going out and spending!   *New York Daily News*, 6 May 2009

No f***ing sympathy here

"Tenacity and ambition overtook me. We thought we could do anything, that we could not fail. We flew too high, too fast."

Motormouth chef Gordon Ramsay tugs at the heartstrings by telling us how he had to sell his Ferrari to aid his ailing restaurant business.

Overcooked

*"It was the worst bollocking ever ... They told me I was f*****."*

Chef Gordon Ramsay again after being told by his auditors that his restaurant empire was on the brink of collapse because he over-expanded.

Allen key to recovery

"I haven't lost any money because I'm terrible. I spend, spend, spend. I am single-handedly keeping the economy going."

Singer Lily Allen discussing the recession and why she's every shop owner's dream!

Press Association Newsfile, 16 May 2009

Seriously Funny Crunchies

Gallows Humour Spawned by the Credit Crunch

Half wit

"This is worse than a divorce. I've lost half my net worth and I still have a wife."

Crocked!

"The Federal Reserve chairman said today that the $700 billion bailout of the banks is not going to be enough money. When did the Federal Reserve become like a car mechanic, you know? 'Yeah, we can get the economy running for maybe $700 billion, but there's no guarantee it's not gonna stall out on you.'"

Jay Leno

"How do you define optimism?
A banker who irons five shirts on a Sunday."

High street banker

"Talked to my bank manager the other day and he said he was going to concentrate on the big issues from now on . . . He sold me one outside KFC yesterday."

Slice of life

"What's the difference between an investment banker and a large pizza? A large pizza can feed a family of four."

Five iron

"How do you define optimism? A banker who irons five shirts on a Sunday."

Growth sector

"The credit crunch is getting bad, isn't it? I mean, I let my brother borrow €20 a couple of weeks back, and it turns out I'm now Ireland's third biggest lender."

Crash policy

"What's the difference between a no-claims bonus and a banker's bonus? You lose your no-claims bonus after a crash."

Economic black hole

"The federal government agreed on Sunday to provide an additional $30 billion to AIG. According to AIG, $15 billion will be used to build the world's biggest toilet, down which the other $15 billion will be flushed."

Seth Meyers

Bargain basement

"Do you have any idea how cheap stocks are now? Wall Street is now being called Wal-Mart Street."

Jay Leno

Bitter pint

"Three bankers go into a pub . . . because that's where they work now."

Down payment

"What's the difference between a banker and a pigeon? A pigeon can still leave a deposit on a Ferrari."

Attention seeker

"Q: In these busy market times, how can you get the attention of your broker?

A: Say, Hey, waiter!"

136

Fund manager

"I went to the ATM this morning and it said 'insufficient funds'
... I'm wondering, is it them or me?"

Car crash

"The credit crunch has helped me get back on my feet. The
car's been repossessed."

Under the mattress

"Sign spotted in the window of an Edinburgh shop:
'Beat the credit crunch – buy your own bank.'
Underneath, the killer line:
'Buy a new mattress from us.'"   The Daily Record, 11 March 2009

Ignorance is bliss

"There are two types of economists: those who cannot forecast
interest rates and those who do not know that they cannot
forecast interest rates."

Back to the future

"Government's view of the economy could be summed up in a
few short phrases: if it moves, tax it. If it keeps moving, regulate
it. And if it stops moving, subsidise it."

Ronald Reagan

Gallows humour

"Q: What is the difference between Iceland (that country that went bust) and Ireland?

A: One letter and six months."

Mop up operation

"The last time Iceland had a crash like this aisle three was closed all day."

Icy forecast

"An Icelander and an American are chatting: The American says: 'Here we got George Bush, Stevie Wonder, Bob Hope and Johnny Cash.' The Icelander says: 'We've got Geir Haarde (Prime Minister); No Wonder, No Hope, No Cash.'"

Soft landing – and take-off

"It isn't so much that hard times are coming; the change observed is mostly soft times going."   Groucho Marx

Biting off more than he can chew

"George Bush was asked today, 'What do you think of the credit crunch?'
He replied: 'It's my favourite candy bar.'"

Mistaken identity

"President Bush said that he is saddened to hear about the demise of Lehman Brothers. His thoughts at this time go out to their mother as losing one son is hard but losing two is a tragedy."

Double standards

"President Bush was in New York City this afternoon. He was giving a speech imploring people to crack down on accounting fraud, lashing out and attacking accounting fraud. And I am thinking to myself, 'Hey wait a minute, isn't that how he got elected?'" David Letterman

Definitions

"Broker: What my stock adviser has made me.
Standard and Poor: Your life in a nutshell."

Diminishing returns

"With the current market turmoil, what's the easiest way to make a small fortune? Start off with a large one."

Closed shop

"Why have estate agents stopped looking out the window in the morning? Because otherwise they'd have nothing to do in the afternoon."

Toxic assets

"The United States have developed a new weapon that destroys people but it leaves buildings standing. It's called the stock market."

Jay Leno

Chaos merchant

"There's a surgeon, an architect and an economist. The surgeon said, 'Look, we're the most important. God's a surgeon because the very first thing God did was to extract Eve from Adam's rib.' The architect said, 'No, wait a minute, God is an architect. God made the world in seven days out of chaos.' The economist smiled, 'And who made the chaos?'"

Merger mania

"3M and Goodyear will merge and become – MMMGood.

FedEx is expected to join its competitor UPS to become – FedUP.

Honeywell and Dewey Electronics – Honey Dew."

Madoff scheme

"Prisoner: 'Lemme get this straight. I give you one cigarette and next week you guarantee me ten?'
Bernie Madoff: 'It's that simple.'"

Newspaper cartoon about Ponzi Scheme criminal Bernie Madoff in prison.

In the cooler

"It's so cold today that Bernie Madoff is actually looking forward to burning in hell." David Letterman

Moving statue

"Bernie Madoff has been charged with swindling people out of $50 billion. I don't want to say he's unpopular, but today as he was walking in New York, he passed a manger scene and Joseph threw a sandal at him." Jay Leno

Backhanded compliment

"In his speech yesterday, President Barack Obama lashed out about these excessive bonuses. He said the trouble at AIG was caused by recklessness and excessive greed. But here's the problem. The AIG executives thought it was a compliment. They went, 'Oh, thanks, wow.'" Jay Leno

Making the cut

"President Obama, getting very tough now, has imposed a $500,000 salary cap for executives getting federal bailout money. And, listen to this: Now on weekends, they can only play miniature golf. No more 18 holes." Jay Leno

Barefaced cheek

"How about this for nerve? This is unbelievable. The porn industry is now asking for a $5 billion federal bailout. The porn industry. Talk about a stimulus package." Jay Leno

Tunnel at the end of the light

"Daylight savings time has started which means we've an extra hour of daylight every day to see your life savings going down the toilet." Craig Ferguson

Car scrappage scheme

"A plan to bail out the Big Three automakers stalled in Congress today. Yeah. As a result, Congress plans to buy a better-built Japanese bailout plan."   Conan O'Brien

Thanks for nothing!

"The stock market keeps going down and down and down. Today I tipped my cab driver with 100 shares of General Motors stock."   David Letterman

Sleep like a baby

"A concerned customer asked his stock broker if the recent market decline worried him.

The broker told him that he has been sleeping like a baby 'Really?!?' replied the customer.

'Absolutely,' said the broker, 'I sleep for about an hour, wake up, and then cry for about an hour.'"

Step down

"I have an uncle who works down at Wall Street. He used to have a corner on the market. Now he has a market on the corner."

Fast fund outlet

"Q: What do you say to a hedge fund manager who can't short-sell anything?

A: A quarter pounder with fries, please."

Tall stories

"AIG says they're trying to raise more money by selling their big office building in New York. It's 66 stories! And not one of them is the truth."   Jay Leno

Cash flow problems

"Money talks. Trouble is, mine only knows one word – goodbye."

Wasting by degrees

"Q: Why are all MBAs going back to school?

A: To ask for their money back."

The Wall Street splash

"Q: What's the one thing Wall Street and the Olympics have in common?

A: Synchronised diving."

Customer decline

"According to a new report, Ford, General Motors and Chrysler have greatly reduced their number of customer complaints. The automakers did this by greatly reducing their number of customers."

Conan O'Brien

Good return!

"In a stunning announcement, Citigroup showed a profit and had its best quarter since 2007. They made $8 billion in profit. That just goes to show you, you give a company $45 billion in government bailout money, and they'll show you how to turn it into $8 billion. See, this is capitalism!"

Jay Leno

Not a leg to stand on

"Resolving to surprise her husband, an investment banker's wife pops by his office. She finds him in an unorthodox position, with his secretary sitting in his lap. Without hesitation, he starts dictating, '. . . and in conclusion, gentlemen, credit crunch or no credit crunch, I cannot continue to operate this office with just one chair!'"

Double whammy

"President Bush was on Wall Street giving a speech on corporate responsibility. He called for the doubling of punishment for corporate crime. That means they will slap you on both wrists, apparently." Jay Leno

Plum job

"Yesterday Federal Reserve Chairman Alan Greenspan said he would be willing to serve another term. Greenspan said, 'Where else would I get a job in this economy?'"

Conan O'Brien

Fitness fanatic

"According to a new study, bad economic times can actually be good for you because people tend to exercise more and eat better. This is not a recession; this is the Bush Health Care Plan." Jay Leno

Déjà vu

"Things do not look good. The economy's gone south, we're at war, people are out of work. In fact, George Bush Sr picked up the newspaper and thought, 'Hey, I must still be president.'"

Jay Leno

Manipulating the market

"People have underestimated this guy. Five months ago he would have had to pay €10 million for that house. But thanks to his economic plan he got it at a bargain."

Jay Leno talking about President George W Bush, after his purchase of a new home in Dallas worth €2 million.

Official mourning

"When George Bush finally leaves the White House, the satire industry will briefly join the rest of the economy in recession."

Comedian Rory Bremner joins the ranks of anxious workers thanks to the demise of George Bush.

Scotland on Sunday, 18 January 2009

Barely with it!

"I'm not so sure that Sarah Palin knows what to do about the economy either . . . She was asked what you should do in a bear market. She said, 'Well, you should shoot it and skin it.'"

Jay Leno

"If all economists were laid end to end, they would not be able to reach a conclusion."
George Bernard Shaw

One liner

"If all economists were laid end to end, they would not be able to reach a conclusion."

European Central Bank boss Jean Claude Trichet quoting George Bernard Shaw.   *Irish Independent*, 27 February 2009

The Messiah

"After a quick meet-and-greet with King Abdullah, Obama was off to Israel, where he made a quick stop at the manger in Bethlehem where he was born."

Jon Stewart, on Barack Obama's Middle East trip.

List mania

"You know it's a credit crunch when . . .
1. *The cash point asks if you can spare any change.*
2. *There's a 'buy one, get one free' offer – on banks.*
3. *Revenue is offering a 25% discount for cash-payers.*
4. *Your builder asks to be paid in Zimbabwean dollars rather than US dollars."*

Begging belief

"I want to warn people from Nigeria who might be watching our show. If you get any emails from Washington asking for money, it's a scam. Don't fall for it."   Jay Leno

Japanese banking crisis

"In the last seven days Origami Bank has folded, Sumo Bank has gone belly up and Bonsai Bank plans to cut back some of its branches. Yesterday it was announced that Karaoke Bank is up for sale and is likely to go for a song. Today shares in Kamikaze Bank were suspended after they nose-dived and 500 back-office staff at Karate Bank got the chop. Analysts report that there is something fishy going on at Sushi Bank and staff fear they may get a raw deal."

Definitions

"A Committee:

1.   *A cul-de-sac down which ideas are lured and then quietly strangled.*

2.   *A group that keeps minutes and wastes hours.*

3.   *The unwilling, picked from the unfit, to do the unnecessary."*

Bright spark

"A director decided to award a prize of €1,000 for the best idea to save the company money during the recession. It was won by the employee who suggested reducing the prize money to €100."

Sheep dog

"A risk manager, walking down a country lane, encounters a shepherd standing near a field of sheep. 'If I can accurately predict the number of sheep in this field, would you let me have one?' asks the risk manager.

'Certainly,' replies the shepherd, having just counted them himself. The risk manager gets out his slide rule, calculates the area of pasture needed to sustain one sheep, estimates the area of the field and comes up with the figure 423.

'That's absolutely correct,' says the shepherd, and the risk manager stoops to claim his prize.

'But,' adds the shepherd, 'You must give me the chance to get even. If I can accurately guess your profession, we'll call it quits.' The risk manager agrees.

'You're a risk manager for a major investment bank,' says the shepherd.

'That's right,' says the bemused manager, 'But how did you know?'

The shepherd replies: 'Give me back my dog and I'll tell you.'"

Broke and broker

*"Bank Manager: 'Get my broker, Miss Jones.'
Secretary: 'Yes sir. Stock, or Pawn?'"*

You're not alone

*"If you think nobody cares if you're alive, try missing a couple
of car payments."*

Earl Wilson

Seeking mortgage approval

"Take the plot of the Ocean's 14 *movie: I can reveal that
George, Brad and the gang pull off the best caper yet – they
tunnel into the vaults of a bank and try to get a mortgage."*

Jonathan Ross

Prudent spending

*"Prosperity is when people buy things they can't afford;
recession is when they stop doing it.*

HE Martz, *The Wall Street Journal,* 1963

School yard humour

"A new teacher was getting to know the kids by asking them their name and what their father did for a living.

The first little girl said: 'My name is Mary and my Daddy is a postman.'

The next child, a little boy said: 'I'm Andy and my Dad is a mechanic.'

And so it went until one little boy said: 'My name is Johnny and my father is a striptease artist.'

The teacher gasped and quickly changed the subject. Later, in the school yard, the teacher approached Little Johnny privately and asked if it was really true that his dad danced nude.

Little Johnny blushed and said, 'No, he's really a Business Development Director at Lehman Brothers, but I'm just too embarrassed to tell anyone.'"

Correct definition

"The stock market crashed this week but they're not calling it a crash. They're calling it a correction. You never hear that at the NASCAR. 'Oh we had a fiery correction on turn 3. Four men are dead.'" Jay Leno

Modern remake

"Do you remember the film Trading Places, *where a Wall Street banker lived on the streets? If they made that now, it would win Best Documentary."*   Jonathan Ross

Unbalanced books

"The problem with investment bank balance sheets is that on the left side nothing's right and on the right side nothing's left."

Illustrated copy

"The rescue bill was about 450 pages. President Bush's copy is even thicker. They had to include pictures."

Dire humour

"Have you heard about the new Dire Straits bank account? Money for nothing, and your cheques for a fee."

154

Our generation

"The Who have rereleased, and reworded, their hit 'My Generation' for the current crisis:

> *People try to bid things down, talking 'bout securitisation,*
> *Just because the market's drowned, talking 'bout annihilation,*
> *All my bonds I hope get sold, talking 'bout remuneration,*
> *Hope I trade before I get old, talking 'bout my termination,*
> *My expectations, or humiliation baby?*
> *In my situation I need medication baby!"*

It's no fun!

"The crunch has hit fairgrounds. My friend lost his job as a Dodgems operator today. He's suing for funfair dismissal."

Three for two

"Latest three-for-two offer at Boots: sun cream, hairspray, bank."

Solid financial advice

"I'd like to start a small business. How do I go about it? Easy, says the bank manager. Just buy a big one and wait."

Recession era junk mail

"I need to ask you to support an urgent secret business relationship with a transfer of funds of great magnitude . . .

I am Ministry of the Treasury of the Republic of America. My country has had crisis that has caused the need for large transfer of funds of 800 billion dollars US. If you would assist me in this transfer, it would be most profitable to you . . ."

Penny apples

"A young man asked an elderly rich man how he made his money. 'Well, son, it was 1932. The depth of the Great Depression. I was down to my last penny, so I invested that penny in an apple. I spent the entire day polishing the apple and, at the end of the day, I sold that apple for ten pennies. The next morning I bought two apples, spent the day polishing them and sold them for 20 pennies. I continued this for a month, by which time I'd accumulated a fortune of £1.37. Then my wife's father died and left us £2 million.'"

Definition

"Profit: An archaic word no longer in use."

Economic nosedive

"Brian Cowen, Brian Lenihan and Mary Coughlan are flying to an economic summit. Brian Cowen looks at Lenihan and chuckles:

'You know, I could throw a €50 note out of the window right now and make one person very happy.'

Brian Lenihan shrugs his shoulders and says: 'Well, I could throw five €10 notes out of the window and make five people very happy.' Brian Cowen says: 'Of course, but I could throw ten €5 notes out of the window and make ten people very happy.'

The pilot rolls his eyes, looks at all of them, and says: 'I could throw all of you out of the window and make the whole country happy.'"

"It's not based on any particular data point; we just wanted to choose a really large number."

US Treasury Department Spokesperson

Global Banking Crunchies

Wall Street Horrors

Accurate forecasting

"It's not based on any particular data point; we just wanted to choose a really large number."

A US Treasury Department spokeswoman explaining how the $700 billion figure was chosen for the economic bailout.

Forbes.com, 23 September 2008

Liquidity issues!

"It's like peeing in your pants. It feels good but only for a short time."

Annika Falkengren, CEO of Seb, on Baltic devaluation.

Euromoney magazine, June 2009

Man of few words

"It can be summed up in one word: it is a dreadful mess."

BBC business editor Robert Peston even has trouble with maths in these troubled times.

Just about sums it up

"An economist is an expert who will know tomorrow why the things he predicted yesterday didn't happen today."

The late Laurence J Peter, quoted during the current financial crisis. *The Mail on Sunday*, 22 June 2008

Long-term excuses

"A long-term investment is a short-term investment that has gone horribly wrong . . ."

Lots of investors have been boasting about their long-term investments of late! *The Sunday Times*, 27 July 2008

Calm before the tsunami

"It's quite possible that at some point we may get an odd quarter or two of negative growth, but recession is not the central projection at all."

In May 2008 Mervyn King, Governor of the Bank of England, wasn't too bothered about the "r" word.

Oops!

"The facts changed, and the facts justified a big change in bank rate and we made it."

By November 2008 it was fasten your seat belts time for Bank of England Governor Mervyn King and the British public!

Something to look forward to!

"Not since the First World War has our banking system been so close to collapse. The long march to boredom and stability starts tonight."

Mervyn King says we face a long journey through recession.

The main street crash

"A collapse in US stock prices certainly would cause a lot of white knuckles on Wall Street. But what effect would it have on the broader US economy? If Wall Street crashes, does Main Street follow? Not necessarily."

US Fed Chairman Ben Bernanke saying that the subprime fallout would be "contained".   *Afterquotes.com*

Mr Complacency

"At this juncture, the impact on the broader economy and financial markets of the problems in the subprime market seems likely to be contained."

The US Federal Reserve Chairman Ben Bernanke is still sticking to his guns! This is what he told a US Congressional hearing in March 2007.

You as well!

"A once-in-a-century credit tsunami . . ."

Alan Greenspan, the former Chairman of the US Federal Reserve, wades in with maritime explanations for the crisis.

The Times, 24 October 2008

Presumption of innocence

"I stated, 'We're here to find out if there's an innocent explanation.' Madoff said, 'There is no innocent explanation.'"

Reported comments of Bernie Madoff, who was convicted of a $50 billion Ponzi Scheme fraud, after a call from a polite FBI agent to his house.

Rules aren't rules

"In today's regulatory environment it's virtually impossible to violate rules."

Bernie Madoff in 2001. The writing was on the wall back then!

You wouldn't understand …

"It's a proprietary strategy. I can't go into it in great detail."

The clues were there as far back as 2001 when Bernie Madoff was describing his trading approach.

Quoted in *The Independent*, 1 January 2009

Multi-tasker

"It's amazing how he could look people in the eye and have dinner with them and all the while he was stealing their money. He has ruined people's lives."

Victim of Bernie Madoff.   *The Sunday Times*, 21 December 2008

Let him swing!

"Twelve years would be okay if he spent them hung by his toes."

A victim of financier Bernie Madoff after hearing he's looking for a twelve-year sentence for his crimes.

NBC News, 24 June 2009

Lucky for some

"Somebody had to get a little lucky with him."

A New York construction worker, Ralph Amendolaro, who used swindler Bernie Madoff's prison number to play the lottery and won $1,500.

The New York Daily News, 29 March 2009

Unhappy endings

"I believed it would end shortly and that I would be able to extricate myself and my clients from the scheme. This proved difficult and, indeed, impossible."

Bernie Madoff on his $50 billion Ponzi Scheme.

Sunday Tribune, 15 March 2009

We're fine!

"Dick Fuld is very conscious of risk ... He's created a culture that's enabled us to do fine."

Doomed US bank Lehman Brothers vice-chairman Thomas Russo. The bank was dangerously exposed because of subprime mortgage debt.

Quoted in the *New Zealand Herald*, 30 December 2008

What doesn't kill us makes us stronger

"We have been through adversity before and we always come out stronger."

The CEO of Lehman Brothers Dick Fuld attempts to convince the world that the bank will be just fine! Fuld's last compensation package totalled $34.4 million.

Nothing to worry about!

"We have a long track record of pulling together when times are tough ... We are on track to put these last two quarters behind us."

Lehman Brothers CEO Dick Fuld. Anger was directed towards Fuld because he earned $300 million in compensation in eight years.

Quoted in *New Zealand Herald*, 1 January 2009

Rumour machine

"I believe that unsubstantiated rumours in the marketplace caused significant harm to Lehman Brothers."

Lehman Brothers CEO Dick Fuld puts Lehman's demise down to rumours.   *The Sunday Business Post*, 28 December 2008

Scapegoat!

"When I find a short seller I want to tear his heart out and eat it before his eyes while he's still alive."

Dick Fuld.   Quoted in *The Independent*, 1 Jan 2009

$480 million question

"Your company is now bankrupt, our economy is now in a state of crisis, but you get to keep $480m. I have a very basic question for you: Is this fair?"

Congressman Henry Waxman grilling Lehman's boss Dick Fuld.
Quoted in *The Independent*, 1 January 2009

Blame the weather!

"A financial tsunami much bigger than any one firm or industry."

Dick Fuld in testimony to a US congressional committee. Not our fault! We've heard that one before.

The Daily Telegraph, 7 October 2008

The global catastrophe ate my homework

"Looking back on my time as CEO, I don't believe AIG could have done anything differently. The market seizure was an unprecedented global catastrophe."

Robert B Willumstad, former CEO of AIG – a massive insurance company which suffered a major financial crisis in 2008. It was the market's fault of course!

The Guardian, 8 October 2008

Grasping at straws

"AIG's attempt to blame accounting rules was 'like blaming the thermometer for a fever'."

Former chief accountant at the Securities and Exchange Commission, Lynn Turner, is more sceptical.

The Guardian, 8 October 2008

Unloved!

". . . the first thing that would make me feel a little bit better toward them is if they'd follow the Japanese example and come before the American people and take that deep bow and say, I'm sorry, and then either do one of two things: resign or go commit suicide."

US Senator Chuck Grassley reacting with outrage to the news that AIG were paying $165 million in executive bonuses.

rawstory.com, March 2009

*"Boy, you thought St Patrick drove the snakes
out of Ireland. Let's send him down to Wall
Street. That's what we should do."*

Jay Leno

You're dreaming . . .

"Some people look at sub-prime lending and see evil, I look at sub-prime lending and I see the American dream in action."

US Senator Phil Gramm from Texas. He's a longtime free market advocate who fought for financial deregulation.

The Guardian, 26 January 2009

Wailing Wall Street!

"When I am on Wall Street and I realise that that's the very nerve centre of American capitalism and I realise what capitalism has done for the working people of America, to me that's a holy place."

Senator Phil Gramm again. You'd need to pray in Wall Street these days all right.   *The Guardian*, 26 January 2009

Snakes on a stock exchange

"Boy, you thought St Patrick drove the snakes out of Ireland. Let's send him down to Wall Street. That's what we should do."

American chat show host Jay Leno has a cunning plan.

Quoted in *The Irish Times*, 20 March 2009

No Stearns warning

"[There is] absolutely no truth to the rumours of liquidity problems."

Bear Stearns statement days before the firm collapsed. The bank collapsed in March 2008 and was sold to JP Morgan.

Cuddly Granddad!

"The only people who are going to suffer are my heirs, not me. Because when you have a billion six and you lose a billion, you're not exactly like crippled, right?"

Bear Stearns chairman Jimmy Cayne – during meetings about bankruptcy.

Bum advice

"Don't begrudge Bear Stearns' Jimmy Cayne and Lehman's Dick Fuld their millions. Let Merrill's Stan O'Neal and Morgan Stanley's John Mack get paid more than Croesus. You heard it here first: they deserve it. In fact, they deserve more than they earn now. Those five men are underpaid because they are about to make you very rich if you buy their stocks."

CNBC's financial pundit Jim Cramer gets it pretty wrong back in 2007.

River bank?

"The crucial principle in future is that if it looks like a bank and quacks like a bank, we better regulate it like a bank."

Adair Turner, chair of the UK Financial Services Authority.

Euromoney Magazine, February 2009

Lock 'em up!

"The issue has gone unanswered for years. What is going on is simple stealing. We don't need new laws against this, we already have them."

Economist Susanne Trimbath gets tough!

Euromoney Magazine, December 2008

Glorious record

"Congress's record of regulating executive pay has been unblemished by success."

Professor Kevin Murphy of the University of Southern California on why bankers are unlikely to have their pay packets and bonuses limited.   *The Irish Times*, 17 October 2008

The forecast going forward . . .

"The European economic forecast is pretty grim. About the only place that doesn't look too bad is Cyprus, and that is really due to money laundering by crooked Russians."

Sir Howard Davies, Director of the London School of Economics and Political Science.

Press Association Newsfile, 28 May 2009

Good news!

"The economic freefall has been stopped, the collapse of the financial system averted."

Billionaire investment tycoon George Soros.

Press Association Newsfile, 12 May 2009

Or is it?

"A single swallow doesn't make a summer. I must admit though I am swallowing hard as the market continues to go against me."

An unnamed trader quoted in *Euromoney magazine*.

December 2008

Get rid of it, quick!

"You can't keep money around forever. It's like saving sex for your old age."

Legendary investor Warren Buffett is an old man in a hurry! He still has good instincts, having made a killing from Goldman Sachs during the credit crunch.

The Observer, 28 September 2008

Managing assets

"There are no bad assets, only misunderstood assets."

Paul Krugman shows his caring side.

The New York Times, 21 March 2009

Cash in the sofa

"A lot of people sitting on cash are happy to be sitting on cash at the moment."

Hong Kong trader Andrew Sullivan with his credit crunch era version of money in the mattress as the markets meltdown continues.
The Irish Times, 11 October 2008

Cash landing

"Cash and foetal."

Advice on the two safest economic positions in current conditions.
The New York Times, 1 October 2008

Global Political Crunchies

Barack, Biden and Brown Battle on!

Complete Lula!

"This was a crisis fostered and boosted by the irrational behaviour of people who were white and blue-eyed."

President of Brazil Luiz Inacio Lula da Silva has some very specific suspects in mind who are responsible for the credit crunch.

Mail on Sunday, 29 March 2009

Buffer zone

"My administration is the only thing between you [CEOs] and the pitchforks."

Barack Obama points out some salient facts to bank executives during a White House meeting.

Politico.com, 3 April 2009

Share of controversy

"By the end of the week he'll be accusing me of being a secret communist because I shared my toys in kindergarten. I shared my peanut butter and jelly sandwich."

Barack Obama on John McCain's allegations against him.
San Francisco Chronicle, 29 October 2008

Speak and spell

"John's last-minute economic plan does nothing to tackle the number-one job facing the middle class . . . as Barack says, a three-letter word: jobs. J-O-B-S, jobs."

US Vice-Presidential candidate Joe Biden spells out government policy – sort of! *ABC News*, 15 October 2008

The History Channel

"When the stock market crashed, Franklin D. Roosevelt got on the television and didn't just talk about the, you know, the princes of greed. He said, 'Look, here's what happened.'"

Vice-Presidential candidate Joe Biden slips up again. FDR wasn't president during the Wall Street crash and nobody had a telly in 1929. Katie Couric interview, 22 September 2008

"He is like some sherry-crazed old dowager who has lost the family silver at roulette, and who now decides to double up by betting the house as well."
Boris Johnson on Gordon Brown

Overexposed!

"We have . . . a naked King Gordon desperately trying to cover his embarrassment over the N-word – nationalisation."

Rather disturbing imagery here. British opposition MP Vince Cable accuses Gordon Brown of a cover-up!

The Observer, 27 January 2008

Slumber party

"So your question is, did I think we would get here and how do you think we will get out of it? We should have all brought our sleeping bags."

Former US President Bill Clinton doesn't miss a chance for a slumber party! Here he's at a conference in Medellin, Colombia, trying to answer a question about the economic crisis. *Euromoney Magazine*, May 2009

Mother Brown

"He is like some sherry-crazed old dowager who has lost the family silver at roulette, and who now decides to double up by betting the house as well."

London Mayor Boris Johnson has been reading a bit too much Dickens. This is his description of UK Prime Minister Gordon Brown.

Some hope!

"*Barack Obama said yesterday that the economy was 'going to get worse before it gets better'. See, that's when you know the campaign is really over. Remember before the election? 'The audacity of hope!' 'Yes, we can!' 'A change we can believe in!' Now it's, 'We're all screwed.'*"

Jay Leno focuses in on a more realistic post-election Barack Obama.

GI Joe

"*I'd like to throw these guys in the brig . . . They're thinking the same old thing that got us here, greed. They're thinking, 'Take care of me.'*"

US Vice-President Joe Biden socks it to the bankers.

The New York Times, 29 January 2009

Small change

"*Finally we got some good news about the economy. Barack Obama got $800 billion to rescue the economy. All I can say is, 'Thank you, Oprah.'*"

David Letterman gets to the bottom of the money trail!

Homeland security

"Barack Obama's mother-in-law might be moving into the White House with him. Joe Biden was right. Hostile forces will test him in the first few months."

Some domestic disturbances lie ahead for Barack Obama, according to Jay Leno.

Blast from the past

"Bank failures are caused by depositors who don't deposit enough money to cover the losses due to mismanagement."

Former Vice-President Dan Quayle with his Ladybird book explanation for the banking crisis – which has now been revived.

Gardener's world

"You can grow your way out of recession; you can't cut your way out of it."

British Chancellor Alistair Darling is getting out the Baby Bio and compost to grow the British economy.

The Albanian model

"We expect GDP in Albania to grow by about 6% this year. Government spending has been increasing and there have been fewer power shortages thanks to favourable weather conditions."

Seyhan Pencapligil, CEO of Banca Kompetare Tregtare. At least the Albanian economy is growing – and the weather is good!

Euromoney Magazine, September 2008

Barney blarney

''These two entities – Fannie Mae and Freddie Mac – are not facing any kind of financial crisis. The more people exaggerate these problems, the more pressure there is on these companies, the less we will see in terms of affordable housing."

Oops! Democratic Representative Barney Frank of Massachusetts calls it wrong on the two mortgage institutions six years ago.

The New York Times, 11 September 2003

Flying visit

"It's almost like seeing a guy show up at the soup kitchen in high hat and tuxedo. It kind of makes you a little bit suspicious."

Congressman Gary Ackerman, on the big three US carmakers arriving in a private jet to beg the government for financial aid.

Dating game

"Market to Obama. I'm just not that into you."

Commentator James Pethokoukis abandons clichés like green shoots and instead opts for chick flicks to explain market turmoil.   *The Washington Times*, 8 March 2009

Can we?

"There's still time to turn this around. But Mr Obama has to be stronger looking forward. Otherwise, the verdict on this crisis might be that no, we can't."

Economist Paul Krugman on the stimulus package, 2009.

Stimulating point

"What do you think a stimulus is? It's spending – that's the whole point! Seriously."

US President Barack Obama.

marketwatch.com, 5 February 2009

Wise words

"A recession is when your neighbour loses his job. A depression is when you lose yours."

Ronald Reagan during the 1980 presidential campaign.

Same difference

"We're not in a recession. I don't think we will go into a recession. We're in a slowdown, and there's a difference."

US President George W Bush is slow to recognise the dangers. *The Sunday Times,* 2 March 2008

Possible is nothing

"Americans . . . still believe in an America where anything's possible – they just don't think their leaders do."

Barack Obama.

No fair!

"Why did the financial collapse have to happen on my watch? . . . It's just pathetic, isn't it, self-pity?"

US President George Bush during his final White House press conference. *Time* magazine

So that's what happened!

"There's no question about it. Wall Street got drunk. . . . It got drunk and now it's got a hangover."

President Bush, speaking at a Republican Party fundraiser, gives us his unique take on the credit crunch. So that's what they mean by liquidity.   *The Boston Herald*, 27 July 2008

Suck off!

"If money is not loosened up, this sucker could go down."

Yet another example of George Bush's brilliant grip on economics.   *The Sunday Times*, 28 September 2008